WHERE DREAMS COME TRUE

The Daily Cruise Letter/The Daily Cruise News

Captain Pappas reports that it should be fine sailing as we make our way from Corfu to Naples. Since this is our only full day at sea, why not make the most of it?

Start your day off with a light breakfast at the Garden Terrace while you gaze out at the turquoise waters of the Mediterranean. Join a spinning class in our fitness centre or "salute to the sun" in a yoga session on the Helios deck. Refresh yourself in the Mermaid Lagoon and Coral Cove, or just lounge poolside with a good book. Our full-time librarian, Ariana Bennett, will be happy to make recommendations.

Don't forget to check the special offers in our gift shops, then relax to the soothing music of our pianist in the opulent Court of Dreams. Join the captain for a champagne reception at La Belle Epoque, followed by dinner in the Empire Room. It's baccarat night at Caesar's Forum, but if gambling's not your thing, come up to the Starlight Theater at ten o'clock and discover how romantic a movie can be under a glittering night sky.

Mediterranean days and Mediterranean nights. Yours to experience on *Alexandra's Dream.*

CINDY KIRK

learned at an early age the value of having an active imagination. If she didn't like the ending of a television show or movie, she simply thought of a different one. Or if she had difficulty falling asleep, instead of counting sheep, she made up a story. When she was sixteen she penned these words in her diary, "I don't know what I would do if I couldn't be a writer."

But it would be several decades before her dream would become a reality. Now a wife and mother, Cindy is a writer of contemporary romance. She invites you to get to know her by reading her novel and visiting her Web site at www.cindykirk.com.

Mediterranean NIGHTS™

Cindy Kirk

THE TYCOON'S SON

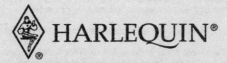

HARLEQUIN®

TORONTO • NEW YORK • LONDON
AMSTERDAM • PARIS • SYDNEY • HAMBURG
STOCKHOLM • ATHENS • TOKYO • MILAN • MADRID
PRAGUE • WARSAW • BUDAPEST • AUCKLAND

ISBN-13: 978-0-373-38962-9
ISBN-10:   0-373-38962-0

THE TYCOON'S SON

Dear Reader,

Writing a continuity book was a new experience for me. When I was asked to write *The Tycoon's Son* I was thrilled and told editor Marsha Zinberg that she'd picked the perfect book for me. I love all kinds of animals, so Theo's work to help the wild horses of Kefalonia touched a chord in my heart. Theo and Trish were also such great characters that it was a pleasure helping them find their happy ending.

Getting to know the other authors involved in the MEDITERRANEAN NIGHTS continuity was also a wonderful experience. They are a talented group of women and I can't wait to read all the other books in this series!

Best,

Cindy Kirk

To author Patt Marr, who seems to know everyone—probably because she is so much fun to be around! I owe Patt a big thanks for introducing me to Greek woman extraordinaire Pam Dokolas, who helped me with all things Greek. Anything Greek I got right in this book is thanks to Pam. Any errors are strictly my own.

DON'T MISS THE STORIES OF

Mediterranean
NIGHTS™

CHAPTER ONE

TRISH MELROSE FELT like a hooker. Or maybe a college student at the end of a bar crawl…

It wasn't even one o'clock in the afternoon and here she was sitting in a taverna with a carafe of Greek wine on the table in front of her.

Okay, so maybe she didn't look like a lady of the evening. Her skirt brushed her knees and the linen shell beneath her suit jacket didn't show a bit of cleavage. And, as far as the coed thing, the fine lines at the edge of her eyes weren't usually found on a college girl's face.

But that didn't change the fact that for the past thirty minutes she'd been sitting in the small café in Corfu Town, sipping the same glass of wine and plastering a smile on her face whenever the tiny bells above the door jingled a new arrival. With unabashed interest she'd checked out every man who walked through the door.

She only prayed Theo Catomeris wouldn't keep her waiting much longer.

As the owner of a growing company in Miami that arranged shore excursions for cruise ships, Trish loved everything about her job…except the games.

While arriving late was a common way to show power, in this case it was totally unnecessary. Theo Catomeris had to know that he was the one in control.

If he said yes to her very generous offer, billionaire Elias Stamos would be appeased and Trish would retain her firm's contract with Liberty Line.

Unfortunately if he said no…

Trish's fingers tightened around the wineglass. She didn't want to think about what would happen if she failed.

There was so much at stake. If she lost the Liberty contract she'd have to lay off or cut back the hours of at least one of her two employees. Who would it be? Twyla, the single mother who gave 110 percent every day? Or James, whose wife didn't work and who'd just bought his first house in anticipation of the baby due next month? Her company, Excursion Plus, was more than just a business. She and her employees worked hard but they also had fun. And they all cared about each other. She couldn't let them down.

Maybe if she groveled…

She stopped the thought before it could go any further, appalled it had even crossed her mind. Trish Melrose didn't grovel. Had never groveled. Would never grovel.

She would do her best to convince Mr. Catomeris that it would be in his—and his wildlife foundation's—best interest to continue to do business with Liberty Line. She'd make the points she'd rehearsed calmly and rationally.

The offer she had for him was a win-win. If he renewed his contract with Liberty Line for excursion services—the same services he'd been providing to Liberty passengers prior to the cruise line's buyout by Argosy Cruises, Trish would make a hefty donation to his pet project, a foundation to help the wild horses of Kefalonia.

In actuality the money for the donation would come from Elias Stamos, the owner of Argosy Cruises and now Liberty Line. But the Greek billionaire insisted she leave his name out of the offer. As far as Theo Catomeris was concerned, Trish's company would be the one making the donation. She'd asked several times why the subterfuge was necessary but had never gotten a straight answer.

When she'd seen she was getting nowhere, Trish had checked out the legalities with her attorney and discovered doing it the way Mr. Stamos required was perfectly legal. Only then had she finally agreed to do it his way.

Now all she needed to do was convince Catomeris to sign.

If he ever showed up, that is.

What if he'd forgotten?

That seemed unlikely considering she'd confirmed the meeting by e-mail just yesterday.

Did I mix up the time?

It couldn't be that. When *Alexandra's Dream* had docked off the small Greek island this morning, Trish had made sure her watch was on local time. She'd double-checked her notes for the location and had arrived at the small taverna on the edge of the Esplanade at precisely twelve-fifteen…well ahead of their twelve-thirty appointment.

The arched colonnade lined with cafés at the edge of the vast main plaza and park had practically begged to be explored. But today wasn't about shopping and sightseeing. The meeting with Theo Catomeris was her priority.

Trish had already discussed this issue with him once. Shortly after she'd learned he hadn't signed the new agreement with Liberty, she'd e-mailed him, assuming the contract had gotten lost in the mail…or on his desk. His response had been brief and to the point. *Not interested.*

She'd immediately started looking for other vendors. But Stamos had insisted on Theo Catomeris. So Trish had tried again. She'd followed up the e-mail refusal with a call. The connection hadn't been good but there'd been no misunderstanding the response. Catomeris had made it more than clear he wasn't interested in working with the new owner of the cruise line.

Mr. Stamos hadn't been happy with the news but he'd given Trish one more chance. She would join one of his cruises, and when the ship docked in Corfu, she would meet with Catomeris and make her plea in person.

The action seemed extreme—personally she would have just replaced Catomeris—but Elias Stamos was the client and it was his call.

"You no like the food?"

Trish looked up to find the proprietress's anxious gaze fixed on the nearly full plate and glass in front of Trish.

Menka was short and nearly as round as she was tall. Her long hair, more silver than black, pulled back from her face in a fat bun. Trish guessed her to be somewhere in her late seventies.

Trish offered her a reassuring smile. She'd always had a soft spot in her heart for older people and Menka clearly went out of her way to make her customers comfortable. Though the woman's English was far from flawless, she was easily understood. In fact, when Trish had first arrived, they'd spent several minutes bonding over discussions of Miami, where Menka had relatives.

"I like the food very much." To illustrate the point and further reassure the woman, Trish took a sip of wine and popped a piece of feta into her mouth.

She must have been convincing because Menka

patted her on the shoulder and moved on to the next table.

Glancing around the café, now half-filled with diners, Trish was suddenly happy that Catomeris had chosen this place to meet instead of one of the upscale restaurants or European bistros surrounding it.

The small, family-owned taverna had a warm, homey feel that had instantly put her at ease. Intricately tatted lace topped the oilcloth covering the tables, and the lamps scattered throughout the dining area gave the café's interior a golden glow. It was almost like meeting in a favorite friend's living room.

The bells heralding another new customer pulled Trish from her reverie. She shifted her gaze to the doorway just in time to see Menka wrap her arms around a broad-shouldered man.

With his dark curly hair, aquiline nose and classic cheekbones, the man standing just inside the doorway could have posed for the Greek statue on the cover of the travel guide nestled in Trish's purse. Not only that, but he was in the age range of the man Trish had come to meet.

Trish straightened in her seat, her senses on high alert. Could this be Theo Catomeris?

He glanced around the room. When he saw Trish, she offered him a smile. Instead of returning the friendly gesture, he turned and spoke to the proprietress again. Menka shook her head and pointed to

Trish, obviously reiterating that she was the only American in the room, or perhaps the only one waiting for someone.

As he started across the taverna, Trish took the opportunity to study him. Like her, he was dressed for business. Anticipation quickened Trish's pulse. Since starting in the cruise industry fifteen years ago, she has discovered her ability to exhibit a cool confidence under pressure had served her well. After becoming her own boss five years ago, she'd been successful in contracting with most major cruise lines to provide excursion services to their guests.

Not to say it hadn't been challenging. Every day other companies sprang up promising to do what she did…only better, faster, cheaper. In the highly competitive travel industry, she'd had to develop nerves of steel. But this wasn't just another industry executive she was dealing with, this was a man whose decision could cause her to lose a significant percentage of her current business.

Apparently determined to make her wait, the man stopped at several tables, taking time to laugh and talk with other patrons. Customers called out in Greek to him or raised a hand in greeting. Trish decided the fact that most of the people here knew him probably wasn't all that surprising considering the size of Corfu Town.

Finally he stood tableside. Trish rose to her feet and extended her hand. "Theo Catomeris?"

"Mrs. Melrose." A slight smile touched his lips and he gave her hand a brief shake. "It's a pleasure to finally meet you."

His English was perfect with only the barest hint of an accent.

"Please," she said, taking his hand. "Call me Trish."

A tingle raced up her arm when her palm met his large callused one in a firm grip. Up close his brown hair reminded her of strong coffee, so dark it could almost be black. But the hint of gray at his temples told her he wasn't as young as she'd first thought. In fact, he was probably a little older than her own thirty-seven years.

Still, he was a magnificent forty. A man in his prime. She could practically feel the waves of testosterone rolling off him.

"You may call me Theo," he said politely, pushing in her chair as she took her seat.

Out of the corner of her eye, Trish saw a few people staring and realized she and Theo had become the main attraction in the small café.

"Have you had lunch?" she asked when he took the seat opposite her.

Mentioning food or the weather was always a good conversation starter. But Theo didn't have a chance to respond because the proprietress chose that moment to deliver a bottle of ouzo to the table along with ice and water. The older woman's cheeks might have been a road map of wrinkles, but her dark eyes still had a youthful flare and a healthy dose of curiosity.

"This woman is a friend, Theo?" the woman asked, her hands fluttering in the air like tiny wrens.

"Mrs. Melrose and I have done business together in the past," Theo said smoothly. "She and I have some work-related concerns to discuss."

Theo went on to introduce the proprietress as his grandmother, Menka Catomeris. He also casually mentioned that his grandfather, Tommy, was in the kitchen cooking.

After a few seconds of polite conversation, the woman bustled off to take care of other diners. But not before giving Theo another hug and making him promise to stop in back and see his grandfather before he left.

Trish felt a pang of envy. It was obvious the threesome had a warm, loving relationship.

"You're lucky to be so close to your grandparents," Trish said, her tone sounding wistful even to her ears. It had been her dream to have her daughter, Cassidy, grow up surrounded by family. But her ex-husband's parents were too busy with their own lives to spend much time with the child and Trish's parents lived in Nebraska.

Theo poured ouzo into the glass and added water. "They're more like parents than grandparents. I've been with them since I was a baby."

She'd expected him to continue but his lips clamped down as if he'd said more than he'd intended.

"I'm sorry." A wave of compassion washed over Trish. "Did your parents die?"

"No." Theo raised the glass to his lips. "My mother lives in Athens. My father isn't…involved."

Trish almost asked what had happened, but at the last minute regained her common sense. This was a work-related luncheon, and until their business was concluded, it wouldn't do to let the conversation get too personal. Still, the more she knew about Theo, the better she'd be able to solidify a deal that met both their needs.

"How did you get started doing tours?" she asked.

"I went to college in Athens," he said in an off-hand tone, taking a sip of ouzo. "Then to Stanford for my MBA."

Trish smiled. No wonder he spoke such perfect English.

"And then?" she prompted when he didn't immediately continue.

"When I returned to Greece, I worked in Athens for a brokerage firm for several years." His eyes grew distant with remembrance. "But my heart wasn't in it. I bought my first boat, returned to Corfu and started my business."

Trish picked up a piece of feta. "How many boats do you have now?"

"Six," he said, a note of pride in his voice. "We now go to most of the Ionian Islands. In the beginning it was just Kefalonia."

Trish took another bite of the delicious cheese, and tried to get a hold on the excitement strumming through her body. The excursion to Kefalonia was the reason for this meeting, and Theo had just opened the door to that discussion.

"From what I understand, Kefalonia is a must-see for visitors to this area," Trish said, doing her best to keep her tone casual.

"You've never been there?" Menka asked, suddenly reappearing to place a plate of savory phyllo pastries on the table. Apparently the older woman had decided if they were there, they were going to eat.

Trish shook her head. "This is my first visit to the area."

"You must go," Menka said. "You must make a tour."

Trish hesitated. She and her friend had booked a spot on an excursion to Kefalonia later in the afternoon. But she hated to mention the plan for fear Theo would use it as a reason to cut their meeting short.

"It sounds like Kefalonia is a place everyone

should have a chance to see," Trish answered instead, casting a pointed glance toward Theo.

Theo nodded. "It's very beautiful."

"Theo. Maybe you could—" Menka stopped mid-sentence, her gaze focused on Theo. Instead of continuing with the thought she merely patted Theo on the shoulder and scurried off.

Theo glanced down at the phyllo pastries his grandmother had placed on the table. "Yiayia likes to bring me all my favorite dishes when I come here. I can ask her for a menu if you'd like to order something else."

"Thank you, but these will be fine. They look wonderful." The delicious smells in the café had set her stomach to rumbling and she'd always found eating to be conducive to doing business. "While we're eating, why don't you tell me a little bit about Corfu?"

Theo obligingly started talking and continued to talk while Menka brought them salads and then grilled fish. It didn't take Trish long to realize why Theo was so effective as a tour operator. The man possessed a wealth of knowledge about his home country…and a passion.

Yet by the time the galactoboureko—a milk custard pie with phyllo pastry and a touch of honey—had arrived, Trish had lost interest in geography and history.

Instead she found her attention focused on Theo. On the way his brown—almost black—hair brushed his shoulders. The way his lips closed around the spoon with the custard, the way he gestured with his fingers to make a point.

Even the way he talked fascinated her. His English was excellent, but occasionally his inflection would reveal that he wasn't a native speaker.

Trish suddenly wished that she didn't have an agenda and could just enjoy his company. If only the words *business* and *contracts* didn't have to cross her lips.

She wasn't sure how he was going to react to the incentive she planned to offer him. Regardless of what Mr. Stamos called it, offering Theo's foundation a generous donation in exchange for him resuming the Kefalonia excursions smacked of bribery.

"Trish." Theo's deep voice broke through her reverie and she looked up to find him staring at her, an inscrutable expression on his face.

"I suppose you want to get down to business." She practically sighed the word and a dimple flashed in his cheek. Once she'd laid the offer on the table, the delightful lunch would be over.

He leaned back in his chair. "What's on your mind?"

Trish opened her mouth and the words she didn't want to speak tumbled out.

CHAPTER TWO

"COULD YOU EXPLAIN to me," Trish said, lifting a glass of ouzo to her lips, "your reservations about signing the contract to do shore excursions for Liberty Line?"

Though Theo had wondered how long it would take her to get to the point of the meeting, disappointment coursed through him. He'd been enjoying her company and hated to see the conversation turn ugly.

He had terminated all of his tour company's contracts with the Liberty Line when his father had bought out the previous owners.

He had no doubt that Mrs. Melrose, Trish, was in league with his father. When he'd spoken with her on the phone she'd been careful to portray herself as an independent businesswoman who needed his help. But Theo hadn't been fooled. Her new alliance with Elias Stamos made her the enemy.

But he'd contracted with her company for a number of years and had always been treated fairly. That was the only reason he'd agreed to meet with her. *Not* because he was considering her offer, but out of respect.

"The previous owners of Liberty were friends of mine," Theo said, meeting her gaze. "I don't care to work with the new owner."

"Is that what you want me to tell Mr. Stamos?" Trish's voice remained calm but the two bright patches of color on her cheeks told him he'd been right to delay this discussion. At this point, the only way their conversation was going to end was badly.

"Tell him whatever you want," Theo said with a careless shrug.

"There has to be more going on here." Trish's brows pressed together in a delicate frown. "In our business we both work with people we either don't know very well or sometimes don't particularly like. As long as they follow the terms of a contract, I don't see the issue."

She was a bulldog, this one. Once she'd latched on to something, it wouldn't be easy to shake her loose. But this was one battle that wouldn't be won by tenacity, because Theo would never, *ever* work for the man who had abandoned him as a boy, no matter how pretty the emissary.

"You don't need to understand." A thread of steel wove its way through Theo's voice. "All you need to know is that I don't choose to accept your offer."

Trish opened her mouth to speak but shut it without saying a word.

Theo felt a surge of satisfaction. She'd finally

gotten the message. And she'd taken his refusal remarkably well. His gaze lingered on her face, the ivory skin with a smattering of freckles, the patrician nose with just enough tilt to make it interesting. If she were just another tourist from America, he'd ask her to go with him to Kefalonia this afternoon.

Visitors to the island were always awed and amazed at its beauty. If they'd had time, he might have even taken her up into the mountains and shown her the wild horses...

"I understand there are wild horses on Kefalonia," Trish said.

Theo jerked back slightly. It was as if she'd read his mind.

"I don't know if I told you," Trish said. "But I'm a huge animal lover."

Theo tilted his head. It confused him when women switched conversation topics midstream. Usually he could follow their logic...but not this time.

"Is that right?" He wrapped his hands around the steaming cup of espresso.

"I'm involved with Paws and Hands Together," she said. "It's a shih tzu rescue organization."

Theo pulled his brows together, trying to place the breed. "Are those the dogs that look like mops?"

Trish laughed. "They're the ones."

"What do you do with the organization?" He liked the way her eyes lit up when she talked about the dogs.

"I maintain the Web site," she said, the tension which had tightened the corners of her mouth easing. "And I take in foster dogs, ones waiting to be adopted. I also do some fund-raising. Finding good homes for these animals takes some serious cash."

The passion in her voice was contagious and suddenly Theo found himself telling her all about the wild horses of Kefalonia and his plans to save them from extinction.

"I can't believe that the government isn't doing more to protect them." Outrage filled Trish's voice and her hazel eyes flashed.

Theo had to smile at her vehemence. He felt the same way but had learned anger without action accomplished nothing. "I know what you mean. We continue to lobby for a ruling to protect wild horses on public and National Park lands. But we can't wait for that to happen. We need to focus on making changes happen ourselves."

"That can get expensive."

There was something in her voice that caused him to look up. But all he saw on her face was concern.

"It is," Theo admitted. "We need to improve the watering facilities and provide shelter, as well as developing nature watch facilities and protection safaris. It all costs money."

He leaned forward and his love for these abandoned creatures welled up and spilled over into his voice. "The wild horses of Mount Ainos have no one else. If my foundation doesn't help them, who will? They are on the verge of extinction."

His grandfather had taken him to Kefalonia for the first time when he'd been but a small boy. They'd hiked the mountain above the village of Arginia and it was there that Theo had gotten his first glimpse of the ponies.

When his grandfather had told him that no one wanted the proud, spirited animals, Theo had felt an instant affinity. Though he knew his grandparents loved him, sometimes he felt as if no one wanted him, either.

Way back then, when he'd been but a child, he'd vowed to help the horses.

Now his childish dream had become a reality.

"Where do most of your donations come from?" Trish's voice pulled him back to the present.

"Ironically, from tourists." Theo gave a little laugh. "When we do our tours…when the visitors watch the horses gallop across the steep, rocky slopes of the mountain, they fall in love. And when they learn of the precarious fate of these beautiful animals, they dig into their wallets."

The generosity of the Americans, in particular, continued to amaze Theo.

Trish's finger traced an imaginary figure eight on the tabletop. "It sounds like fewer tours to Kefalonia could mean less money for your foundation."

There was something in her way-too-casual tone that sent red warning flags popping up in Theo's head. "What are you trying to say?"

Trish looked straight at him. "By refusing to contract with Liberty, it would seem that you are also cutting off a large source of potential donors to your foundation."

The statement hung in the air, bold and raw, for several heartbeats. Theo tightened his grip on the cup. "I'm not contracting with Liberty."

Trish leaned back in her seat and expelled a long breath. "If you look at this rationally—"

"I've said all I'm going to say on the matter," Theo told her, not bothering to hide his irritation. He'd given her his answer. The subject was not up for discussion.

To his amazement, Trish didn't back down. She leaned forward and rested both elbows on the table. "Hear me out," she said, raising a hand when he started to speak. "I really want you to sign that contract. It will be good for me, good for you, and—"

"I told you—"

"—and good for your foundation," she continued without missing a beat. "As a bonus for signing I will donate the following sum of money to your foundation—"

Theo's jaw dropped open at the amount she named. It was at least a year's worth of tourist donations. For a second his mind jumped ahead to what they could do with the money. They could start work on some additional self-filling watering facilities, they could—

No. He shut down the wishful daydreams playing in his head. Even if he was interested in signing— which he wasn't—there was something about the offer that didn't ring true.

"What do you say?" she asked, her eagerness making her words come out fast. "The way I see it, this deal is a win-win for everyone."

She looked so pretty sitting there with the sunlight from the window dancing across her hair and a hopeful gleam in her eyes that Theo was hard-pressed not to give her everything she wanted.

"This money you would donate," Theo said, "where would it come from?"

She paused for a half heartbeat before answering. "From my company."

The momentary hesitation confirmed Theo's suspicions. Still he pressed onward, wanting to hear her admit that his father was behind this offer. "It's a large sum."

"My business is important to me. Keeping clients such as Liberty happy and satisfied is essential." There was an earnest look on her face and a ring of truth in her words. Still, Theo wasn't convinced.

"Stamos gave you the money, didn't he?" Theo

suddenly leaned forward, crowding her, trying not to be distracted by the intoxicatingly sweet scent of her perfume.

She averted her gaze, her hair hiding her eyes from view. "I told you," she said, "I will be the one writing the check."

He wasn't fooled. She still hadn't answered his question. "But the money will come from him."

"How many times do I have to tell you." A hint of desperation crept into Trish's tone. "I will be—"

"The money is coming from him." Equally determined, Theo hammered his point.

"Do you really care who it comes from?" Trish gazed at him over the top of her glass of ouzo, a splash of red coloring her cheeks.

Disappointment coursed through Theo's veins. It was as he'd thought. The redheaded American was in league with the devil. She didn't care about the horses…or him. All she wanted was to get him to bend to his father's will. Theo pushed back his chair. "Our business is concluded."

"You didn't give me your answer," Trish protested.

"I'd sooner strike a deal with Satan himself than enter into an agreement with Elias Stamos," Theo said, keeping his tone low, aware of the curious glances directed their way.

Confusion clouded Trish's gaze. "But why? I'd say in this instance he's being more than fair."

"I don't like to be manipulated," Theo said. "And I don't like lies."

Her cheeks reddened as if she'd been slapped. She lifted her chin and her eyes blazed, but when she spoke her words were carefully measured and conciliatory. "I'm sorry you feel that way. That's certainly not the intention of the offer." She leaned forward, resting her forearms on the table. "I want to help you and the wild horses. At least consider the possibility."

Theo could see the desperation in her eyes. She obviously had a lot at stake here. But he couldn't help her, not this time.

His mind had been made up long ago, when he was a little boy. Back then he'd vowed never to have anything to do with the father who hadn't wanted him.

And that was a promise he intended to keep.

CHAPTER THREE

TRISH STARED at the three wild ponies on the hillside and breathed in the fresh mountain air. The brilliance of the blue sky wrapped itself around her and the sun warmed her face. She'd scheduled the side trip to Kefalonia so she could better understand why Elias Stamos insisted this excursion be offered to his passengers.

It made sense now.

As far as Trish was concerned, the history and beauty of Kefalonia was something everyone should experience. The plight of the horses was something everyone should know, and no one told their story better than Theo Catomeris.

She turned from the wild ponies and slanted a sideways glance at the handsome Greek. She wasn't sure which of them had been more surprised when she and her friend, Sally Edwards, had shown up at the dock for the three-thirty tour.

Right now his attention was focused on a salesman from Cincinnati. But during the boat ride from Corfu to Kefalonia, and even on the trip in the van to Mount Ainos, she'd caught him slanting quick glances at her. Trish could only hope her presence would prompt him to reconsider her offer.

Mentally crossing her fingers, she turned back to the horses, watching in amazement as one—a spunky roan—negotiated a steep patch of rocky hillside with surprising ease.

"Incredible," Trish breathed.

"I know," Sally said. "If he didn't have that bald spot in the back, he'd be perfect."

Bald spot? Although the ponies weren't close, Trish had a good view of the roan and, from where she stood, his hair appeared intact.

"What bald spot?" Trish asked.

"Shh." Sally grabbed her arm, and when she spoke, her voice was a whisper. "He'll hear you."

Trish rolled her eyes. Okay, so maybe she spelled words she didn't want the dogs in her home to hear, but the pony was so far away she could have shouted without worrying about the animal being offended.

"The horse is not going to hear me," Trish said. "And even if he did, I hardly think he's going to care."

"Horse?" Sally's perfectly tweezed brows pulled together. "I'm talking about Jerry."

Aha. Finally Trish understood. Jerry Arthur was the salesman Sally had been flirting with since they'd met on the boat ride from Corfu. Recently divorced,

Jerry was in the Greek Isles on business. He was also the one currently monopolizing Theo.

Trish cast a surreptitious glance in their direction. "You're right," Trish said to Sally. "The guy does have a bald spot."

"I'm not criticizing, mind you. I think it makes him look distinguished." Sally's lips curved up in a satisfied smile. "Did I tell you he promised to look me up the next time he's in Omaha?"

"That's great, Sal." Trish tried to put some enthusiasm in her voice. While she wanted to believe the man would call, she had the feeling this was the last her friend would see of the guy. It had been her experience that men often promised things then didn't deliver.

Sally and Trish had been best friends growing up in Nebraska. They'd kept in touch even after Trish had left for college in Florida. Though still single, Sally had never given up on her dream of having a husband and children.

Two years ago, at age thirty-five, Sally had decided to make her dream a reality. She'd lost eighty pounds, bought some new, stylish clothes and lightened her mousy-brown hair to blond. While she would never be model-thin, her weight loss had given her a newfound confidence with men and she'd jumped into the dating scene with an enthusiasm Trish envied.

"I'm glad you made me go on this excursion,"

Sally said, her blue eyes sparkling. "I wouldn't have missed this for the world."

"I can't imagine missing this, either." Though Trish didn't endorse his tactics, she now understood why Elias Stamos wanted this excursion available to his passengers.

Trish had barely finished speaking when Theo's voice rang out over the crowd.

"If you all move closer, I'll tell you about efforts currently underway to save these fine animals." His deep voice sent a shiver up Trish's spine. Though he'd made it clear when they'd left the taverna that their business was concluded, Trish couldn't help but hope the door was still open.

She began to move forward, and when she turned to say something to Sally, Trish found herself alone. Sally now stood next to Jerry, her arm looped casually through his.

Trish sighed and let the group of people push her forward until she stood directly in front of Theo. His lips were moving ever so slightly, and it took Trish a second to realize he was counting, making sure all twenty-five people in the tour group were present.

She waited with anticipation for his gaze to settle on her. But when he got to her, he skipped over her.

The action told her more than words that the door was still shut.

Theo took a step back and gestured with an outswept arm toward the side of the mountain and valley below.

"This mountain where we now stand is Mount Ainos. Below you can see the village of Arginia. And if you look over there, you can see three of the wild horses of the island." Though his voice never faltered, Trish could see the emotion in his eyes when he looked at the horses. "These animals belong to a mountain breed of Greek horse descended from the Pindos breed. The Pindos is a descendent from the old Thessalonean breed which is now extinct."

Though a few in the crowd moved away, most were as mesmerized as Trish by the passion in Theo's voice as he painted a vivid picture of the horses' struggle to survive.

"While they have faced tremendously adverse conditions in the past, these horses now face even greater challenges. They share this area with many other animals. Years ago, there was enough food and water for all. Now, due to the felling of many trees as well as destructive fires, the horse's ability to find enough food and water is threatened."

"What can we do to help?" the distinguished-looking older gentleman next to Trish called out.

"Thank you for asking," Theo said. "We've established a foundation to save these horses. The imme-

diate goal is the provision of self-filling watering facilities and shelter, along with a balanced diet in the
winter months."

Theo didn't stop there. He went on to talk about
more extensive long-range possibilities before mentioning to the group that when they stopped at the
Monastery of Zoodohos Pigi on the way down, they
would have an opportunity to make a donation, if
they so desired.

After giving them a few minutes to take pictures,
Theo announced it was time to head back to the van.
As they started down the mountain path, Trish fell
into step beside Theo.

"We're going to have to stop meeting like this,"
she said, keeping her tone deliberately light.

This time Theo couldn't ignore her. "I didn't know
you were coming on this tour."

Trish struggled to keep up with his fast clip. Normally she loved hiking, but she'd tripped on a hidden
rock on their way up the mountain and her ankle was
still sore from the almost fall.

Theo must have noticed her difficulty because he
slowed his pace and even reached out a helping hand
when she stumbled.

"I guess we're even then," she said.

"How's that?" he asked.

"I didn't know you were going to be leading
this tour."

He shot her a skeptical glance.

"I didn't," Trish said. "When I booked the tour, someone named Basil was listed as the guide."

"Basil went home sick," Theo admitted. "I'm filling in for him."

"You do a nice job," Trish said. "When you were talking about the hardships the horses face…"

Her voice caught. She wondered if the bay or the gray or the black roan would die this winter. Trish took a moment to compose herself. Ever since she'd been a child she'd loved animals. While her encounters with horses had been few, these proud, well-spirited ponies had found their way into her heart.

She thought of the money Elias Stamos would give, and how it could make the difference in these horses surviving the winter…or not.

While Theo hadn't been overly friendly, he hadn't been hostile, either. Maybe now that he'd had time to think, he'd be willing to take the money and give these horses a chance at a better life. She simply *had* to try again…

"I was wondering if you'd thought more about my offer," Trish said.

A tiny muscle jumped in his jaw. "No," he said. "I haven't."

It might not have been the most encouraging answer she could have gotten but it gave Trish something to build upon.

"I know," she said. "There hasn't been much time. It seemed like I'd barely left the taverna to meet Sal when it was time for the tour to start."

"Sal?" He stopped and turned to face her.

He stood so close Trish could see the sheen of sweat on his brow and she realized his eyes looked more gold than brown in the light. Her heart did a little flip-flop in her chest.

"Sal?" he repeated.

"My friend." Trish gestured with her head toward the back of the group. "The blonde."

"The woman with Larry," Theo said, his eyes dark and inscrutable.

"Jerry," Trish said, automatically.

Theo's gaze remained fixed on hers. "Is he a friend of yours, too?"

Trish frowned. Why were they talking about a salesman from Cincinnati when they had more important things to discuss…like Theo accepting the money so the wild horses could survive.

"Sally and I just met him this afternoon," Trish said impatiently.

"I didn't know you were in Corfu with a friend."

"That's not important." Trish wished he'd quit talking and listen to what she had to say.

He started walking again and the road came into view. Time was running out. Dear God, they were almost to the van.

"Theo." She grabbed his arm. "Please. There's something I have to say to you."

He hesitated only a second before stepping off to the side and letting the rest of the group follow the trail to the van.

"You want to apologize." It was more a statement of fact than a question.

"Apologize?" Trish shook her head, suddenly confused. "No, I want you to reconsider my offer."

"Offer?" A hardness edged the word.

"The bonus if you sign the agreement." Trish spoke quickly, sensing a wall was on its way up. When she'd walked away from Theo earlier, she'd told herself she'd done her best. She'd asked. He'd said no. But this was no longer just about her. This was about the ponies. "Think of all the good you could do for these animals with that kind of money."

He opened his mouth then closed it. Trish felt a surge of hope.

"New watering stations," she said in her most persuasive tone. "Grain and other feed to last them through the winter." She leaned close. "Enough money to ensure that no horse will have to die this year."

A moment of longing crossed his face before his lips firmed. "*If* I agree to work with Elias Stamos."

"*If* you agree to resume doing excursions for Liberty Line," Trish clarified.

He waved a dismissive hand. "Same thing."

A puzzle piece clicked into place. "It's him. He's the reason you won't sign. You have something against Elias Stamos."

She asked only out of curiosity. He'd made it clear he wasn't going to do the excursions. While that didn't bode well for her agency's bottom line, Trish had survived tough times before and she would again.

"I gave you my answer." Theo's words were accusatory. "But instead of respecting that decision, you come on this excursion and interrupt my business for the sole purpose of getting me to change my mind."

The idea was so ridiculous Trish couldn't help but laugh. "You make it sound as if I'm stalking you."

She expected him to laugh, too. Or at least crack a smile. But her words were met with a chilling silence. This conversation was going from bad to worse.

"Mr. Catomeris?" An older woman tapped Theo's shoulder. "Will there be restrooms at our next stop?"

"Yes, ma'am," Theo answered politely.

The woman looked at Trish. "Miss, your friend said to tell you she's saving you a seat in the back of the van."

"Thank you." Trish smiled, then heaved a sigh of relief when the woman scurried off.

"I should get back to the group," Theo said, but surprisingly he made no move to leave.

Trish shared his reluctance, knowing this was probably the last time they would be alone. Once she boarded the ship tonight, she would sail off to the next port and he would remain in Corfu.

"Goodbye, Mrs. Melrose," he said finally.

"Goodbye…Theo." Trish reached into her pocket and pulled out the business card she'd forgotten to give him earlier. "If you change your mind or just want to talk about the offer some more, I hope you'll give me a call."

Theo hesitated for only a moment before his fingers curved around the card she held out. "I won't change my mind."

"I understand you feel that way now," Trish said. "But sometimes things change. Just remember I really want your business. I think we'd make a great team."

"You don't give up, do you?"

"The contract is important to me," she said. "Now that I've seen them, helping these horses is important to me, too."

"We need to get to the van," he said. "So you can get back to the ship on time."

Okay, so he hadn't said he'd do it. But given time she knew she could persuade him. Unfortunately time was the one thing she didn't have.

CHAPTER FOUR

AT SLIGHTLY BEFORE eight o'clock in the evening the harbor area in Corfu Town teemed with tourists. Many of them, exhausted after a day of tours and shopping, stood quietly, waiting to get back on the ship. Theo took his place at the end of the line.

Not in the mood to converse, he popped in some earbuds and let the music drown out the conversations around him. If only he could block out his thoughts as easily. But no matter how he tried, Theo couldn't get Trish's face out of his head. All the way down the mountain, every minute of the boat ride back to Corfu, he'd felt her eyes on him.

There was something about the woman that got under his skin. Coming on his tour, for example, had taken a helluva lot of nerve. And then approaching him again with that offer...

He stepped onto the gangway of *Alexandra's Dream*, the flagship of Liberty Line. It had been a long day and it was going to be an even longer night.

This evening he would meet his half sisters, Katherine and Helena Stamos, for the first time.

Theo's looked up at the brightly lit ship. His mother thought he was crazy. Of course, she hated everything to do with Elias Stamos, including his children by his now-deceased wife, Alexandra.

The fact that Alexandra had enjoyed the life which Anastasia had thought should have been hers only fueled his mother's bitterness. She was adamant that Theo have no contact with any of them.

But Theo was curious. Curious what they were like. Over the years he'd seen them on television many times so he didn't think he'd have any trouble recognizing them. But what was there to talk about? They didn't move in the same social circles or share the same lifestyle. And why had they even contacted him? A sliver of dread crawled up Theo's spine.

His mother had been right. Having anything to do with the Stamos family was a mistake. For the briefest of seconds Theo considered leaving. But he'd given his word and, just like a handshake, his word meant something. Besides, he hadn't gotten to where he was by running from difficult situations.

He paused halfway up the gangway and removed the earbuds, slipping them into his pocket. Sounds of music and laughter spilled over from the upper deck. The ship was supposed to pull out in the morning. This was one of those overnight port stays intended to give the passengers more time to enjoy Corfu Town by night.

He continued up the gangway behind a couple of chattering women. When he reached the top, he hesitated. Katherine had said she'd be there to meet him at eight. But it was already five after and there was no woman waiting. Only two staff members screening the returning passengers and a security guard sitting on a chair stood between him and the entrance to the ship.

His tour operator's license had gotten him this far but it wouldn't be enough to get him on board.

"Welcome back," one of the staff said with a smile. "Your boarding pass, sir?"

Theo shook his head and offered an easy smile. "I'm not a passenger. I'm meeting—"

The man's smile disappeared. "I'm sorry, sir. Only passengers are allowed on the ship."

"I understand that," Theo said amiably. "However, I'm here to meet—"

"It doesn't matter, sir," the man said.

"But—" Theo began.

Out of the corner of his eye he saw the guard stand. He wasn't surprised. Because of security concerns, most cruise ships were reluctant to allow non-passengers on board. That's why Katherine was supposed to be here, to navigate him through security.

"I am so sorry I'm late."

Theo heard the feminine voice even before the beautiful woman rounded the corner. Stylishly slim with light brown hair and a fair complexion, she looked more like her English mother than her Greek father.

"Gentlemen, it's my mistake," she said, in a soft, melodious voice. "I planned to be here with this before he arrived but I was detained."

She showed the man the security pass and he scanned it then waved Theo forward. Katherine waited until they were in the hall before wrapping her arms around him in an impulsive hug that seemed to surprise her as much as it did him. He stiffened but didn't pull away.

Her arms dropped to her side and she took a step back then held out her hand. "By the way, I'm Katherine."

He took her hand in a brief shake. "Theo Catomeris."

"Thank you so much for coming." The merest hint of pink touched her cheeks. "And just so you know, I'm not in the habit of hugging complete strangers. But the resemblance to…well, the resemblance is uncanny."

Theo had seen Elias Stamos on television many times. He knew he bore a strong resemblance to the man, but in his family that was never mentioned. He didn't know how to respond to Katherine's comment so he remained silent.

"I'm so happy you decided to come." Katherine

punched the elevator button then gave a nervous laugh. "I think I already said that before, didn't I?"

Theo just lifted a shoulder in a slight shrug. This was a difficult situation for all of them to navigate. At least she was talking. His ability to make small talk seemed to have vanished.

"I was surprised to get the invitation," Theo said finally. "I wasn't aware you knew I even existed."

"Well, I…we…haven't always known," Katherine said. "But we do now."

Theo sensed she shared his unease on how to manage the situation. Obviously meeting your father's bastard son wasn't something covered in most etiquette books.

"Have you had dinner yet?" she asked.

Theo shook his head.

"Good," Katherine said, and he could almost see a little of the tension ease from her face. "Helena and I considered having dinner brought to the penthouse but we thought you might enjoy seeing some of the ship. The Empire Room is the main dining room."

Her speech had taken on a nervous, edgy quality that he found oddly reassuring. At least he wasn't the only one stressed over this meeting.

Katherine took a deep breath and continued. "It serves international cuisine so I'm sure you'll find something to please your palate. It's very impressive."

"Spoken like a true PR person," Theo said before he could stop himself.

Surprise skittered across Katherine's face. "You know what I do?"

"Just what I read in the papers," he said. "I know that Liberty is one of your firm's biggest accounts."

"Well, right now you seem to have the advantage," Katherine said. "Because I don't know a whole lot about you."

"Not much to know." Theo hoped dinner didn't deteriorate into a question-and-answer session. The last thing he wanted to do was spend the evening being grilled about his past. Of course, enduring an hour of awkward silences didn't hold much appeal, either.

They stepped into the elevator and Katherine punched the button for deck five. "Helena will join us there."

"Is Helena younger or older than you?" Theo knew the women had been born a couple years apart but found it hard to keep the two straight in his mind.

"She's thirty-five." Katherine brushed a strand of hair behind her ears with a perfectly manicured fingernail. "I just turned thirty-seven. Sometimes I can't believe I'm that old."

"I'm forty," Theo said. "By your calculations, I guess that makes me ancient."

"Sometimes I feel like all the good years are

behind me." Katherine's expression turned pensive. "Other times it's as if the best is yet to be."

"I understand what you mean," Theo said, feeling a moment of connectedness with this stranger. At twenty, when Theo had envisioned his life, he'd been determined to have it all; a successful business and a loving wife and children. Lately he'd started to realize he'd been so focused on building his empire that the home and family he'd wanted had never materialized. Now he was forty years old, with nothing to show for his life except a fleet of boats and a profit and loss statement firmly in the black.

He shoved the self-pitying thoughts aside. He had a good life, and like Katherine, he held fast to the thought that the best was yet to come.

When the door to the elevator opened, Theo followed Katherine out and down a long hall. A throng of well-dressed men and women were milling around the entrance to the dining room, waiting to be ushered to their table. Theo wasn't surprised when Katherine skirted the crowd.

The maître d' led them to a table draped in white linen in an alcove just off the main dining area. The table looked like something from a magazine with its crystal wineglasses, shiny silver and fine china plates.

Theo didn't give the elegant table setting much more than a passing glance. Instead his gaze settled on the attractive-looking woman with dark hair and eyes sitting at the table sipping a glass of wine. She rose when he approached the table. Unlike her older sister, Helena's hair, eyes and facial features reflected her Greek heritage.

Though Theo wasn't a fashion expert, Helena's brightly colored dress had a designer look. Thankfully her smile was as open and welcoming as her sister's.

She stood and extended her hand. "I'm Helena."

He shook her hand, but instead of releasing it she held it firmly and took a step back. She studied him for a long moment, much as Katherine had, a look of utter astonishment on her face. "You look so much like—"

"He does, doesn't he?" Katherine said, nodding her agreement.

Theo's stomach tensed. Hopefully this would be the last remark he'd have to endure about Elias Stamos. If not, it was going to be a short evening indeed.

He offered an affable smile and gestured at the large airy room, hoping to change the subject. "This is a beautiful restaurant."

"Thank you," Katherine said. "It took a lot of planning. We have a fabulous French chef who is very talented. Excellent cuisine in an elegant environment is all part of giving passengers a memorable dining experience."

Katherine sounded, Theo thought, very much like a proud parent.

"So I know that you're responsible for Liberty's

public relations," he said to Katherine, then turned to Helena. "And you do costume designing for stage and film?"

"That's right," Helena said with a pleased smile. "You've done your research."

"Actually," Theo said, "all I need to do to keep up is read the newspapers and watch television. Your father is an important man and the news media love his daughters."

The minute the words left his mouth Theo saw the look of surprise on Katherine's face when he'd deliberately not claimed any tie to their father. She seemed to be searching for a way to comment when one of the waitstaff standing a discreet distance away moved forward to pull out their chairs.

Once they were comfortably seated, it was Helena, not Katherine who spoke. "What business are you in, Theo? Katherine told me it has something to do with shore excursions?"

"That's correct," Theo said. "My company provides excursions to most of the islands around here. We contract with the major cruise lines so we keep busy year-round. Once we get the tourists to the different locations we have a number of employees on each island to lead tours."

Though his operation had grown considerably over the last few years and earned a nice profit, it was tiny compared to Elias Stamos's holdings. Still Theo couldn't keep the pride from his voice. His company was something he'd built from the ground up, with no help from anyone.

"It must be wonderful to have that much control," Helena said. "When I do my costume designs, I have a lot of artistic freedom but I certainly don't have the final word."

"Remember that show you did in Athens last year?" Katherine asked.

That was all it took for Helena to launch into a diatribe about the director from hell.

Theo just listened, grateful when the server came around and filled the wineglasses. The women were both friendly and going out of their way to make him feel at ease. Still, it seemed awkward to sit across the table from them and know that some of the same blood that flowed through their veins flowed through his. To know that they'd grown up in a whole different world based solely on the fact that his father had chosen to marry their mother.

Still, they kept the conversation going throughout dinner, and just as he'd hoped, the women seemed willing to carry the brunt of the conversation.

He learned that Katherine's husband was an architect with worldwide clients, and consequently his job demanded a lot of travel. He also discovered that Katherine's daughter, Gemma, was on the ship as a volunteer in the children's centre. Helena touched briefly on her failed marriage and satisfaction with her career and single status.

But neither brought up the reason they'd contacted him, and even after they'd finished dessert, he still wasn't sure why he was really there…until a spot of red hair caught Theo's eye.

Trish Melrose, a woman he hadn't planned on seeing again, sat across the dining room at one of the large round tables. His blood turned frigid as he made the connection.

He'd taken Katherine's phone calls, hardly questioning the fact that out of the blue she'd decided it was time for them to meet. He hadn't balked when she'd asked if he'd come aboard *Alexandra's Dream*.

Now he realized he'd been a naive fool. His mother had been right. Katherine and Helena had their own agenda.

Now that he'd discovered what it was, he just had to decide what he was going to do about it.

CHAPTER FIVE

IF ASKED, TRISH couldn't say exactly when she first became aware Theo was in the dining room. All she knew was that right in the middle of her Lobster Newberg, the hairs on the back of her neck prickled. She glanced around, checking out the other tables in her vicinity, but came up empty.

Then, after she ordered dessert, a curious warmth filled her body and she knew with absolute certainty that Theo's eyes were on her. She couldn't explain *how* she knew because she didn't understand it herself.

Taking a sip of cappuccino, Trish slowly scanned the upper level of the dining room. Only this time she cut a broader swath, delving into the farthest reaches of the room, into the small alcoves reserved for VIPs and couples who wanted privacy.

She'd almost surveyed the entire room when her breath caught in her throat. For several heartbeats she sat frozen, unable to look away.

Theo Catomeris, the man she'd thought she'd never see again, sat at a table with two women, one with dark hair, the other an almost-blonde. He looked serious, his expression grim. Trish couldn't help but wonder what they were talking about and why he was on the ship.

When he'd dropped her and the other tourists back in Corfu Town, she'd been certain she'd failed. Now it looked as though she may have been given another chance to convince him to sign that contract with her company. Trish's heart fluttered in her chest and she placed the cup back on the saucer with a trembling hand as excitement coursed through her.

Although she often got an adrenaline rush before making a big business deal, this felt like something more. She suspected her mounting excitement wasn't just because she had another chance to make the deal or save the jobs of her employees. Some of the rush came from seeing Theo again.

"I really wanted Bananas Foster," Sally said with an exaggerated sigh. "But the fruit should be good, don't you think? And it'll be a lot less calories."

"The fruit will be fabulous," Trish heard herself murmur. Pushing back her chair, she rose to her feet and placed her napkin on the table. "I see someone I know. I'm going to run over and say a quick hello."

Without waiting for her friend's reply, Trish started across the dining room, carefully avoiding the waiters holding large silver trays laden with desserts. On her way to Theo's table, she noticed several admiring glances.

She gave all the credit to the russet-colored silk dress she'd picked up several months ago on clearance. It hugged her lithe body, giving a tantalizing illusion of curves where there weren't any.

The closer she came to the table, the happier Trish was that she looked her best. She'd been so focused on Theo that she'd failed to properly appreciate his dinner companions, two very beautiful women in their midthirties.

The one with dark hair and an olive complexion looked as if she could be Greek. The other woman was fair, with classic English looks. Their dresses were designer elegant and judging by the number of waitstaff hovering near the table, one or both were very important.

Interrupting a man having a private dinner is risky, a tiny little voice inside Trish's head warned. *He saw you. He's probably still angry. If he wanted to talk, he'd have come to you.*

Trish knew she could have waited. That may have been a better option. After all, the alcoves were specifically for passengers desiring privacy. But she'd already finished her dinner and she couldn't wait at the table all night hoping he'd come over. Besides, she only planned to say hello. Any business person would do the same.

Drawing closer to the table, she became increasingly aware of the intimacy of the setting. Neither woman looked up as Trish approached. There was something about the threesome...something that was similar. Perhaps it was their shared Greek heritage. Now that she was closer, Trish could see then even though the blonde didn't have the same dark complexion, there was definitely Greek blood in her background.

The dark-haired woman was recounting some tale for Theo, punctuating her words with exaggerated hand gestures. The other woman's attention was totally focused on Theo.

He wore a button-up shirt open at the neck, and its pristine whiteness brought out the olive tones of his skin. Trish could understand why the women couldn't seem to take their eyes off him.

Her steps slowed, but when he looked up and saw her, Trish knew she was past the point of turning back. She was barely five feet from the table when the women finally noticed her.

Of course, Theo pushing back his chair and rising to his feet was a fairly obvious clue that she wasn't just another guest passing by.

"Miss." A tall muscular man in a dark suit appeared out of nowhere and stepped in front of her just before she reached the table. "This is a private party. I must ask you—"

"Mrs. Melrose and I are acquainted," Theo said, cutting off the man's dismissal.

The man kept his feet planted but cast a questioning glance at the fair-haired woman seated to the right of Theo. She inclined her head slightly and only then did the man in the suit step aside.

By now both women were staring, along with the serving staff clustered just a few feet from the table. Thankfully Trish had never been the type to blush. She lifted her chin and extended her hand to Theo. "Forgive me for interrupting. I just wanted to stop by and say hello."

Theo hesitated before his hand closed over hers for the briefest of shakes.

"I believe you know Katherine and Helena." He gestured to the two women at the table, now on their feet and openly assessing Trish.

She blinked several times before she made sense of the strange comment. She couldn't believe Theo was so naive. *Alexandra's Dream* had over a thousand passengers. Just because she and the women were on the same ship didn't mean she knew them. "I'm afraid I haven't had the pleasure." Trish flashed a warm smile and extended her hand first to the dark-haired woman closest to her. "I'm Trish Melrose from Miami, Florida."

The woman took Trish's hand. "Helena Stamos. This is my sister, Katherine."

Stamos? Trish frowned. "Any relation to Elias Stamos?"

Katherine laughed, a light gentle sound. "He's our father. But, please, don't hold that against us."

Despite the words, Trish could hear the fond undertones and knew the woman and her father enjoyed a close relationship.

Theo stiffened and Trish couldn't help but wonder why a man who seemed to have a grudge against the wealthy shipping tycoon was having dinner with the man's daughters?

"Do you know our father?" Helena asked.

"I don't know him personally," Trish said. "I run a company that arranges excursions for cruise lines. So any contact I've had has been on a business level."

Katherine's eyes lit up. "You're the one charged with getting the Kefalonia excursion back on the schedule."

"That's right," Trish said, doing her best to keep her tone light. "I've been trying to convince Theo that it would be in everyone's best interest to sign the contract."

Theo's expression darkened and Trish saw instantly that her calculated risk had blown up in her face.

"But of course, that's his decision to make," she said hurriedly. Trish knew she could stay longer and try to repair the damage, but the tense set of Theo's jaw told her she'd already overstayed her welcome.

"I think it's time for me to get back to my friend. Again, I'm sorry I interrupted." Trish smiled at Theo, not surprised he didn't smile back. "A pleasure to see you again." She turned to Katherine and Helena. "It was very nice to meet you both."

The three resumed their seats. Conscious of their eyes on her, Trish walked away with her head held high, making a determined effort to hide her disappointment. The encounter may have gone badly but she was only down, not out. She would regroup. Plan her next move. She wasn't ready to give up yet.

Still, when she got to the table and saw everyone enjoying their dessert, Trish found herself wishing she'd remained at her table and chosen cheesecake over Catomeris.

"TRISH MELROSE," Katherine mused as she stared after the other woman. "So that's the woman whose company handles the excursions."

"She seems nice," Helena added, casting a sideways glance at Theo.

Theo took a sip of grappa, his gaze still firmly fixed on Trish. When he'd spotted her in the dining room, it had instantly become clear why his half sisters had chosen to eat there. Why he'd been asked to meet them on the ship. Why they'd even contacted him in the first place. He'd been set up. Obviously Stamos had asked them to do their part to get him to sign.

Anger warred with disappointment. Though he didn't know Katherine and Helena well, he'd been open to considering a relationship with them. In his mind, they had nothing to do with their father's treatment of his mother and him. But Trish…well, her behavior shouldn't have been such a surprise. She'd made it clear by her repeated attempts to convince him to sign that her allegiance was with Stamos.

"Theo?" Helena's concerned voice broke through his thoughts. "Is something wrong?"

They'd been in it together. Plotting, throwing out all the stops in an attempt to get him to sign with Liberty. Katherine hadn't contacted him because she wanted to get to know him…she'd done it to help her father. Obviously family loyalty didn't extend to him.

"What's wrong?" Katherine demanded, repeating the question he'd ignored from her sister.

Theo wanted to leave, to head down that gangway and not waste one more minute of time or emotion on either of them. But before he did that, he was going to make sure they understood he knew why they'd invited him on board.

He leaned back in his chair and looked from Helena to Katherine. "Why didn't you just come out and say you wanted me to sign the contract to do the Kefalonia excursion?"

A look of puzzlement furrowed Helena's brow. "What do you mean?"

Katherine took a sip of brandy. "Does this have to do with that woman? With Trish Melrose?"

"She was sent to Greece specifically to pressure me into signing the contract with Liberty," Theo said through tightly clenched teeth. "Your father even gave her money to bribe me."

"It sounds like him," Helena said with a shrug. "The man doesn't understand the word no."

Theo couldn't help the disappointment that coursed through him. Though he'd hardly admitted it to himself, he'd come tonight with cautious hope that he and these women might be able to find some common ground. Now those hopes had been shot to hell.

"You decided to help him get what he wants." Even to his own ears he sounded bitter.

"I don't know anything about excursions." Helena waved a dismissive hand, looking bored with the topic. "I provided input on the redesign of the ship's interior. That's the extent of my involvement. The other stuff doesn't interest me."

But Theo knew it interested Katherine. She was a public relations spokeswoman for the cruise line. And she was the one who'd called him, the one who'd arranged this meeting.

He looked accusingly at her. "You knew, didn't you?"

Katherine tilted her head, her expression giving nothing away. "Knew what?"

"That I hadn't signed the contract."

"Of course," Katherine said with an unapologetic air. "I do PR for Liberty. It's my business to know everything that affects our ability to successfully market our cruises."

Though Theo had made the accusation, it was still disappointing to hear his fears confirmed. "So, I was right."

"Actually," Katherine interrupted, "you couldn't be more wrong. Yes, I knew you hadn't signed the contract, but that had nothing to do with why I called you. Or why I wanted us to get together."

There was a directness about Katherine that Theo had recognized from the beginning. And he felt the first faint stirrings of hope that he might have been too hasty in his judgment. Still, while he preferred to believe that his half sisters genuinely wanted to get to know him better, he had no wish to be played for a fool.

Somehow, he had the feeling that if Katherine had been involved in subterfuge, she'd have been the first to admit it…without making any apologies.

"What about Trish Melrose?" he asked.

"I never saw her before tonight," Katherine replied matter-of-factly. "Though I knew she was on board."

"I didn't even know who she was or what she did," Helena said.

"Although she didn't have anything to do with the

reason I called you, I have to say I do support her efforts," Katherine added. "The excursion to Kefalonia was one of the most popular on this itinerary. I'm not here to push you to sign, but I would be very happy if you did."

What she said made sense. Hoping he wasn't making a big mistake, Theo decided to go with his gut and believe her. "But one thing still isn't clear to me. Why, after so many years, did you call me in the first place?"

"We'd actually thought about doing it for—"

"Ma'am." The man in the dark suit stepped forward. "I'm sorry for interrupting but the captain has announced that all guests need to be back onshore."

Theo glanced at his watch, surprised the evening had gone by so quickly. When Katherine had set up this dinner, he'd thought about the excuses he could give if the time grew long or the meeting became tense and awkward.

Surprisingly he found himself wishing for more time. He'd enjoyed the company of his half sisters far more than he'd imagined.

"The time has gone so fast." Helena leaned forward and placed her hand over his, her eyes intense. "I'm sorry it has to end just when we're starting to get to know each other."

"I wish we had more time, too," Theo said, surprised to find he actually meant it. "Especially since it's impossible to know when I'll see you both again."

"Then don't," Katherine said.

Theo raised a brow. "Don't what?"

"Don't go. Stay on board for the rest of the cruise. We dock in Barcelona in five days," Katherine said. "Consider it a well-deserved holiday."

Theo shook his head. "I've got too much to do to simply take off now. Summer is a busy time."

"It's only five days," Katherine said. "And if you're concerned that you'll be stuck with us 24-7, don't be. While I want to spend as much time with you as possible, this is a working vacation for me. I have a new PR campaign to sort out, and since Charles is away on business—oh, let's be honest. I missed Gemma and wanted to spend some time with her."

"And I'm finishing up some work for a London stage production that will open in the fall." Helena cast a teasing glance at her sister. "Katherine convinced me I could be as creative on the ship as back in my flat, and with fewer distractions."

Katherine looked directly at him. "Now that we've found you, Theo, we don't want to let you go."

A rush of emotion washed over Theo at the simple words. As much as he wanted to believe them, they were, he reminded himself, merely words. And as relatively painless as the meeting had been, he had a company to run. Unlike Katherine and Helena, he didn't have the luxury of changing his schedule on a whim.

No, if and when he saw the two women again, it would be on his terms. And his own time.

CHAPTER SIX

TRISH FINISHED OFF the cheesecake that had been waiting for her and realized she couldn't say if it was scrumptious, horrible, or somewhere in between.

When she'd returned to the table, she'd eaten the dessert automatically, thankful Sally and their fellow diners had been in the middle of a full-blown discussion of the upcoming college football season. She sipped coffee and listened, relieved not to be subjected to any questions about her departure.

She braced herself when the conversation started to peter out, but then the others at the table decided to go to the disco.

It seemed the perfect solution. After all, it was too early to go back to the cabin, and this way Sally could dance and she could strategize. She'd make that deal with Theo…even if she had to get off at the next port and hop on a plane back to Corfu. Perhaps three confrontations—make that meetings—would be the charm.

Once they got to the club, the dentist Sally had

been flirting with all evening asked her to dance. That left Trish seated with the newly married couple who had eyes—and hands—only for each other. Thankfully it wasn't long before they were on the dance floor, too.

Finally alone with her thoughts, Trish stared into her drink, wondering why Theo had acted so cold, so abrupt. Yes, she'd pushed for him to sign the contract, but why the hostility? It felt personal, but this was business. What was she missing? Trish sighed. He was such a difficult man to understand.

Take his dinner companions, for example. It didn't make sense that he would be so chummy with Elias Stamos's daughters yet refuse to do business with the man.

"Would you care to dance?"

Trish jerked her head up and her eyes widened at the sight of a tall dark-haired man in a white officer's uniform. Though they'd never met, she recognized him as Giorgio Tzekas, the first officer.

On the first day of the cruise Sally had deliberately run into the man. Her friend had discovered his name and his position on the ship, but to Trish's knowledge, Sally hadn't seen him again.

And now Sally was busy with the dentist and Trish was sitting all alone feeling sorry for herself. She'd make that contract happen. But it wouldn't happen tonight. And hadn't she vowed to combine business with pleasure on this cruise? She wasn't going to do that sitting alone.

"Sure." Trish flashed the officer a bright smile. "I'd love to dance."

He politely pulled out her chair and followed her to the dance floor. The fast-paced tune was quickly replaced with a slow one, and when the officer's hand slid around her waist, Trish realized they'd skipped introductions. Just because she knew his name didn't mean he knew hers. "By the way, I'm Trish Melrose—"

"I know who you are," he said, pulling her closer.

Trish wiggled back, increasing the distance between them. "You do?"

"I'm a first officer," he said with a wink. "I make it my business to know the names of all the pretty ladies on board."

He stared down at her bosom, and Trish felt uneasy. There was something about this man that she didn't like. He was too confident. Too forward. Too…slimy.

"I saw you in the dining room talking with Helena and Katherine Stamos," Giorgio said then stopped, an expectant look on his face.

The comment came out of the blue and took Trish by surprise. For a second she considered telling the truth; that this was the first time she'd met Elias Stamos's daughters. But she didn't like this man or the fact that it seemed he'd only asked her to dance so he could fish for information.

"Helena and Katherine?" Trish kept her tone non-committal. "Sounds like you know them, too."

She could do a little fishing of her own.

Though the smile remained on his face, Giorgio's hand tensed on her waist. "My father and Elias are old friends. Katherine, Helena and I…we grew up together."

"Yet—" Trish tilted her head "—you work while they play."

"The fault of my father." Giorgio's jaw tightened and he fairly spat the words. "He is a man who believes children should make their own way in the world."

It was clearly a touchy subject. Trish lifted a brow. "I take it you don't agree."

Giorgio opened his mouth to speak then seemed to reconsider. "It doesn't matter," he said finally. "I do quite fine on my own."

They danced in silence for several minutes.

"I couldn't believe they were dining with him," Giorgio said, his voice heavy with disapproval.

Trish resisted the urge to giggle at the man's disjointed way of conversing.

"I don't see a problem," Trish said, wondering what Giorgio had against Theo.

Giorgio looked surprised. "You know who he is?"

"I do," Trish said.

"And you don't see anything wrong with him being on this ship?" Giorgio's voice rose with each word.

"I take it you do." Trish did her best to keep her manner off-hand. He had some point, she just wasn't sure what it was…

"The illegitimate son of Elias Stamos does not belong on this ship," Giorgio said, a muscle along his jawline jumping. "I could not believe Katherine would invite him aboard."

Trish absorbed the first officer's words, stunned. Theo was Elias Stamos's *son?* How could that be?

Suddenly the fog cleared and it all made sense. Theo shared the same last name as his grandparents. His father wasn't a part of his life. That would explain Theo's reluctance to do business with the man. And also Elias's insistence that Theo, and only Theo, do the tours.

Anger rose up inside Trish. No wonder Theo had been so hostile. Elias Stamos had put her in the middle of a family matter. And he hadn't even had the decency to give her the basics…beginning with the fact that the man wanted her to bribe his son.

When she had walked away from Theo's table tonight, Trish had hoped she could find some common ground, address Theo's concerns and come to an agreement. Now that hope was gone. She closed her eyes against a sudden upwelling of regret. There would be no journey back to Corfu. No second or third chance to change Theo's mind.

If Elias Stamos wanted Theo to do his tours, the shipping magnate was going to have to deal with his son himself.

Trish was through being a pawn.

THEO HAD BARELY MADE IT home when his cell phone rang. "*Yasas.*"

"Theo, this is Katherine."

He plopped into the nearest chair and switched to English. "Hello, Katherine."

"You're probably wondering why I'm calling," she said, then continued without giving him a chance to answer. "Helena and I feel strongly that you must join us on this cruise. We're concerned that if you don't, it might be months or years before we get together again."

While Theo was touched they'd called, he didn't have any interest in joining the cruise. "I'm sure the cabins are all booked," he hedged.

"The penthouse is available," Katherine said. "I'll take care of getting your passenger sailing card. I'll even arrange for your flight back to Corfu from Barcelona."

Theo leaned back in the chair and rubbed the bridge of his nose with two fingers. The woman was determined. "I don't know—"

"Theo, this is Helena. Can't you make it work?"

The younger sister's voice turned persuasive. "We're only asking for five days of your life. And the penthouse has a full business center so you can do anything here that you can do in your office, with a lot less distraction."

Normally doing what they asked would be out of the question, but Basil had called as Theo was driving home and said he was feeling better and would be back doing tours tomorrow. Theo considered for a moment. Other than working on some paperwork for a grant, there was nothing on his agenda that couldn't wait until next week.

But did he really *want* to go back to the ship? Was furthering a relationship with his half sisters worth the additional effort and inconvenience?

Theo thought of his grandparents, now in their seventies. His mother had been an only child so he had no aunts, uncles or cousins. Once his grandparents were gone—other than his mother—he'd be alone. If he and his half sisters could forge an amiable relationship, he might have a new family.

All the way home he'd thought about what he wanted out of life, and, as he drove through the darkness, one thing had been crystal clear: he wanted family.

He wasn't sure why—and maybe he wasn't ready yet to probe any deeper—but he wanted his sisters in his life. The longing was so powerful, as if it had always been there inside him, just waiting for him to acknowledge it. "I guess a short vacation never hurt anyone."

Helena gave a little shriek and must have handed the phone back to Katherine because the next voice he heard was hers.

"Wonderful news," Katherine said. "The guard will have your boarding pass when you get here. You'll just have to show some identification."

"When do I need to be there?" Theo asked.

"The sooner the better," Katherine said. "The Captain wants all passengers on the ship by two."

Theo glanced at the clock on the wall. "I'll pack a few things and head back to the dock."

"The card the guard will give you will be your key to the penthouse," Katherine said. "Sleep late and we'll plan on getting together for brunch."

Theo's fingers tightened around the phone. Was he making a mistake? He'd muddled through a couple of hours with his half sisters, but did he really want to be with them for five days? Still, he knew Katherine was right. This could be their only real chance to get to know each other. "Sounds good."

"If you encounter any problems with the guards, have them call me," Katherine added.

"I will," Theo promised. "And, Katherine…"

"Yes, Theo?"

"Thanks for calling."

TRISH LEFT THE DISCO shortly after midnight. Sally was still out on the dance floor with the dentist, doing her own version of the electric slide.

The loud music coupled with her close encounter of the slimy kind had left Trish with a nagging headache. But those weren't the only reasons she'd left the club and headed for the top deck. If she'd calculated correctly, Cassidy should be back at the hotel in Orlando after spending the day at Epcot.

When Trish had learned she'd needed to make this trip, she'd assumed her ex-husband would watch their daughter. Those plans had blown up when Steven announced he'd be out of town on a business trip that week. Thankfully her sister had come to the rescue, offering to take Cassidy on a family vacation to Disney World.

Trish took a seat in a deck chair close to the front of the ship and punched in her sister's number.

"This is Angie."

"You sound pretty chipper for someone who spent the day at Epcot with four children," Trish teased. Her older sister and her husband had three busy little boys ages eight, six and two.

"We actually had a lovely day," Angie said. "Tom bought fast passes so we didn't have to wait in long lines. Cassidy, Brent and Tyler went on all the rides together so all I had to worry about was Ben."

"Thank you for taking such good care of her." To her

surprise Trish found her voice trembling. This was the first time she'd left her daughter for more than a night or two and it scared her to death. "It's so hard to be this far away. But I don't worry knowing she's with you."

Okay, so maybe it wasn't entirely true. She still worried, but that was just the mother in her.

"We're taking good care of your baby girl—" Angie began.

"I'm not a baby," Cassidy called out in the background, the indignant tone bringing a smile to Trish's lips.

"I think someone wants to talk to you—" The words had barely left her sister's lips when Trish heard the sweetest sound in the world…her daughter's voice on the other end of the phone.

"I miss you, Mommy."

Trish blinked away the tears that welled in her eyes. "I miss you, too, sweetheart. But it sounds like you're having lots of fun with Aunt Angie and the boys."

"Me and Brent and Tyler went on a roller coaster," Cassidy said, her small voice reverberating with excitement. "Ben couldn't go 'cause he was too little."

"What other things did you do?"

Trish leaned back in the chair as Cassidy prattled on about the rides she'd gone on and the Slurpee she'd spilled down the front of her shirt. A wave of pure happiness washed over Trish. At that moment, she would have given everything to be in Orlando with her daughter, getting hugs from Mickey and oohing and aahing over Cinderella's palace. Especially with the kind of disaster this cruise was turning into…

"Did the man sign the piece of paper?"

The question startled Trish, and for a moment she wasn't sure what Cassidy was asking. Then she remembered she'd told her daughter that she was going to Greece to get Mr. Catomeris to sign a "piece of paper" saying he would do tours for Trish's company.

"No, sweetheart." Trish gentled her tone. "The man didn't want to do the tours."

"He will, Mommy," Cassidy said. "Everyone wants to work for you."

Though Trish appreciated her daughter's unwavering support, she knew the real issue was whether she could get Theo Catomeris to work with Elias Stamos. She knew Theo had must feel insulted that his father had tried to bribe him, but that understanding didn't change the fact that her business would suffer if he didn't sign her contract.

After promising to call Cassidy tomorrow, Trish dialed her office. Since it was after seven in the evening, Florida time, she didn't expect anyone to be there. But she could give her employees an update on voice-mail. Though she believed honesty was best, she still hadn't decided how much to tell them. After all, they'd have to deal with the bad news soon enough.

To her surprise, a familiar voice answered the office's private line. "Twyla? Is that you?"

"It's me." Concern filled the woman's voice. "But why are you calling? Is something wrong?"

"Everything is fine," Trish said reassuringly. "I was just going to leave you an update. I didn't expect anyone to be there this late."

"There were a couple of things we didn't get done today that needed to be finalized," Twyla said. "I volunteered to work late."

Though Twyla didn't say it, Trish knew that being away from the office had put her staff behind. But she reminded herself she was in the Mediterranean for only one reason: to save their jobs.

"And I've done a bang-up job of that," Trish muttered.

"What did you say?" Twyla asked.

Trish realized with sudden horror that she must have spoken aloud. "What did you do with Sam?"

Twyla was a fellow single mother and the sole support and caregiver for a precocious two-year-old son.

"He's here. I picked him up from day care and brought him back to the office with me," Twyla spoke in that upbeat chirpy tone that defined her personality. "Of course we had to drive through McDonald's for a quick dinner on the way."

Trish smiled. Twyla made working late sound like

a fun adventure, but Trish knew the sacrifice she was making. "I really appreciate—"

"Don't give it a second thought," Twyla said quickly. "We're a team. We help each other out."

Trish recognized the words she was always spouting and her throat tightened "Still, I appreciate the extra effort."

"Enough about me. How'd it go today?" Twyla asked. "Did you get Catomeris to sign?"

Twyla was aware of the importance of keeping the Liberty account. She and James were counting on her to close the deal and save their jobs. How could she tell them she'd failed. Not failed, she reminded herself, given up.

"I met him today," Trish said, choosing her words carefully. "While I didn't get a firm commitment, he is thinking about it."

"Well, at least he's considering the offer," Twyla said. "And if anyone can close this deal it's you."

"I'm going to do my best." Trish vowed to figure out another way to contact Theo before she left this part of the world. And she wasn't just going to do her best, she was going to close the deal. Because Twyla's and her son's happiness depended on it.

CHAPTER SEVEN

WHEN THEO HAD ORDERED food to be brought to his penthouse for a late-morning brunch, he'd never expected the staff to turn his deck into an elegant buffet.

Helena and Katherine hadn't seemed surprised at all when they'd arrived, leaving him to assume such extravagance must be the norm in their world. The food tasted as good as it looked and conversation flowed easily throughout breakfast. Still, Theo could tell Katherine had something on her mind.

He'd been watching her closely, and she was definitely more withdrawn than she'd been last night.

"Is something wrong?" Theo asked her pointedly after the espresso had been poured. "You seem preoccupied."

"I'm afraid I have to get off the ship tomorrow in Naples," Katherine said, true regret in her voice. "Father called this morning. He insists I meet him in Athens tomorrow to discuss some last-minute changes in the new publicity campaign we're getting ready to launch."

"You couldn't discuss it over the phone?" Theo

knew it was futile before the words left his mouth. From what he understood, when Elias Stamos called, you answered.

"'Fraid not." Katherine grimaced. "When it comes to business…"

They hadn't really discussed Elias Stamos and Theo had been thankful for that. But now he found himself curious. Could this last-minute meeting in Athens simply be the man's way of cutting short Katherine's time with him? "Did your father know you and Helena were meeting me?"

Helena took a sip of her mimosa. "We told him."

"He was supportive," Katherine said, answering the unspoken question in Theo's eyes.

"That surprises me." He wanted to trust what Katherine had to say but he couldn't help but be suspicious. After all, how could a man who'd spent his entire life pretending he didn't have a son suddenly do a three-sixty?

"For all his faults, family is everything to him," Helena said.

"Not all family," Theo said flatly.

"His refusal to have anything to do with you is puzzling," Katherine observed. "He certainly could have pushed for visitation since he was paying child support, but he never did. I'm not sure why."

Theo frowned. What kind of game was Katherine playing? His mother hadn't received child support.

Money—or lack of it—was the only reason his mother had left him with his grandparents.

Tasia had been far from the perfect mother but she'd never have done something so…selfish. Was Katherine trying to drive a wedge between his mother and him? Or had Elias lied to his daughters, not wanting to lose their respect?

"I was there once when your mother came to see him." Remembrance lit Helena's eyes. "Neither of them knew I was in the house."

"When was this?" Theo kept his tone offhand.

"A couple years ago," Helena said. "She wanted him to publicly acknowledge you as his son and to make sure you shared in his fortune."

"What did he say?" Theo asked.

"He told her that if you wanted a relationship with him, *you* should contact him, he was through dealing with her." Helena's lips quirked up in a humorless smile. "I'd never seen my father so angry. He said he wouldn't be surprised if she'd spent all that child support money on herself, not you."

"Though I'm sure that didn't happen," Katherine hastened to add. "It was just his anger talking."

A band tightened around Theo's chest making it difficult for him to breathe, much less speak. "What happened then?"

Helena bit her lip, suddenly appearing unsure. "She left."

"He never mentioned you directly to us and we didn't feel it was our place to ask," Katherine added. "Not until this spring. He told us Mother had encouraged him to contact you but he never had."

"So your mother knew about me?"

"That's what he said." Helena took another sip of her drink. "I think he wanted us to know he'd always been honest with her. And he insisted that once he met our mother, he'd never so much as looked at another woman."

"You believe that?" Theo asked. These were sophisticated women. It was hard to accept they could be so naive.

The two women exchanged glances and nodded.

"You'd have believed it, too, if you'd seen them together," Helena said, her eyes unnaturally bright. "They were so much in love."

"It nearly killed him when she died," Katherine added with a sad smile.

"That was, what…about ten years ago?" Theo seemed to remember hearing the news of her death around the time of his thirtieth birthday.

Helena nodded.

"Why do you think he waited so long to tell you about me?" Theo asked.

"I'm not sure what precipitated the father-daughter chat," Katherine said. "Unless his recent bout of chest pain brought his mortality to the forefront."

Theo could feel his pulse pick up. He'd never considered Elias might die before he had a chance to tell the man what he thought of him. "He has heart problems?"

"Checked out fine," Katherine said. "Doctor said it was just stress."

"Last month when we told him we were going to give you a call, he didn't object." Helena's dark eyes softened. "We weren't sure how receptive you'd be. After all, you didn't want anything to do with him. But we decided we might as well ask."

"What made you think I didn't want anything to do with him?" Theo asked.

Helena hesitated for a long moment. "You never called him."

Theo didn't respond. A myriad of emotions—too many to sift through now—wrapped their tentacles around his heart and squeezed tight. How could he tell them that he'd spent his whole life believing his mother hadn't been able to keep him because his father had failed to pay support? And hating the man who'd refused to help her?

"Before I leave the ship I'd like you to meet my daughter," Katherine said, apparently deciding it was time to change the subject.

"Gemma's awesome." Helena's eyes filled with pride. "She's my favorite niece."

"She's your *only* niece," Katherine pointed out.

"I'm looking forward to meeting her," Theo said.

Helena began once again to sing Gemma's praises but Theo tuned her out. He had more to think about than a niece he'd never met. Like a mother who'd lied. And a father who'd tried to bribe him.

He'd thought meeting his sisters would give him clarity…instead he'd never been more confused.

THE SUN SHONE HOT and the resulting tingle on her cheeks told Trish it was time for more sunscreen. She'd been relaxing on the Artemis deck for the past hour. Sally had occupied the chair beside her but had just left for her spa appointment.

Taking off her sunglasses, Trish reached into her bag for her bottle of SPF30. She wouldn't stay out too much longer. Because of her fair complexion Trish had learned from an early age to limit her sun exposure.

She squirted lotion into her hand, and while she smoothed it on her cheeks, she checked out what was happening on deck. Most of the passengers were lounging in the sun or cooling themselves in the pool. It was the primo time of day to soak in the sun's rays and the only chairs that didn't have a person or a towel on them were in the shade.

This was the only day-at-sea in the week's itinerary and everyone appeared to be enjoying the opportunity to kick back. When she'd been single, Trish had loved to bask in the sun with a good book. She hadn't had much time for such relaxation since Cassidy was born.

Yet today she'd barely read five pages. Instead her mind had raced. She hadn't been able to get Twyla and James off her mind. When she'd started her business she'd never realized the emotional burden of being responsible for an employee's well-being. The more she thought about her staff, the more she realized that she couldn't give up. It didn't matter that Elias and Theo were father and son. That fact was just one more obstacle to overcome. She simply had to come up with a plan to convince Catomeris to sign the contract. Period.

She needed a strategy. The standard e-mail or phone call would get her nowhere. Trish was reminded of her mother's favorite saying—if you do what you've always done, you'll get what you've always got.

Well, if she harbored any hope of getting Theo to work for Liberty, she needed to think outside the box.

But being creative, she was discovering, wasn't always easy. Not when you were a woman who'd operated a certain way all your life. She could present the pros and cons of a proposal in a professional, per-suasive manner. She could negotiate a contract and have everyone leave the table feeling like a winner. But being thrust in the middle of a family feud demanded she step up her game and try something innovative.

The sound of a young girl's laughter drew Trish's attention. For the past half hour, children had been arriving for supervised activities in the pool.

Many of the children were close to Cassidy's age and for a second, tears of longing had filled Trish's eyes. She could hardly wait for tonight when she could call her daughter again and hear that sweet little voice.

She smoothed the last of the lotion on her neck and watched a man approach one of the teenage attendants. Trish gasped. Although the man had his back to her, he was built exactly like Theo Catomeris—tall and broad shouldered with lean hips and muscular legs. His dark curly hair brushed the top of his shirt.

But it couldn't be him—Theo had left the ship last night. Trish had asked around, knowing it would be easier to get him to change his mind if he was on board. One of the waiters had told her that Theo had left the ship shortly after the Captain announced all passengers must go ashore.

Though she wasn't into being a voyeur, Trish couldn't stop staring at him. She watched the man give the girl's shoulder a squeeze and turn to leave. Trish widened her eyes. It *was* Theo and he was getting away.

Trish scrambled to her feet, knocking over the suntan lotion in her haste. She didn't give the bottle a second glance or even take time to pull on the little skirt she wore as a cover-up over her bikini bottoms. Fearing her opportunity would be gone if she didn't hustle, she grabbed her bag and scurried across the deck. She reached him just as he got to the automatic glass doors leading inside.

"Theo," she called. Though she wasn't at all winded, her breath came out in short puffs.

At the sound of his name he turned, startled, then stared appreciatively at her bikini-clad body.

Trish closed her eyes for a second. Talking to a former business associate wearing nothing but a few scraps of fabric was an unsettling experience, but Trish determinedly shoved aside her embarrassment.

"I saw you by the Mermaid Lagoon—the smaller pool." She lifted her chin and flashed him a bright smile. "Thought I'd say hello."

"Good afternoon." Though Theo didn't immediately say more, at least he didn't walk away.

"What were you doing there anyway?" It really wasn't Trish's business, but she needed to keep him talking until she thought of a plan.

"Katherine's daughter, Gemma, works with the ship's children's program," he said in an offhand tone. "Katherine wanted me to meet her."

Trish couldn't hide her surprise. "You've never met her before?"

Theo's eyes gave nothing away. "Never had the pleasure."

How odd that he hadn't met his teenage niece until now. Obviously the family wasn't close. Trish filed away the information for future reference but knew better than to say more on the subject. His closed expression told her his family relationships—or lack of—weren't something he wanted to discuss.

"I thought you left the ship last night," Trish said, deliberately steering the subject in a different direction.

"I did." Theo glanced down at her chest briefly. "I came back."

Adrenaline kicked Trish's pulse into overdrive. She wasn't sure what caused her intense reaction. Was it the waves of heat she felt rolling off him? Or was it because finding him on the ship gave new life to her plan to save her employees' jobs? "Are you going to be around for the rest of the cruise?"

She held her breath and prayed. *Say yes. Say yes.*

"I'm not sure," he said. "I came back to spend time with Katherine and Helena. But Katherine informed me this morning she has to leave the ship tomorrow. I may get off in Naples, too."

"Tomorrow?" Trish's heart sank. That wouldn't work at all. She needed time to come up with a plan. Time to convince him signing the contract was a good idea. "You can't leave."

"Excuse me?"

"You need a vacation."

A skeptical look crossed his face. He glanced at the door as if plotting his escape from this crazy woman who was talking nonsense.

"Everyone needs a vacation," she said, attempting to improvise and be clever and doing a horrible job of both. "Especially you."

It wasn't really her fault the attempt was so pathetic, maybe even a bit insulting. It was difficult to think with him standing so close.

"What do you mean, *especially me*?"

Trish offered him a mysterious smile. Obviously she was more quick-witted than she realized. She'd intrigued him and he'd finally stopped looking as if he was ready to flee.

"Come and sit in the sun with me," Trish said. "I'll tell you."

She didn't wait for his answer but turned and headed back to the chairs she and Sally had staked out by the Coral Cove, the outdoor pool.

Though she didn't look back, she sensed his hesitation. Still, she hadn't gone more than a foot or two before she heard his footsteps. All the way across the deck Trish was conscious of Theo behind her.

Her skin prickled and she felt flushed. She wished she'd taken time to put on the skirt. Though she was dressed no different than most of the women around the pool, she suddenly felt exposed and more than a little self-conscious. She picked Sally's book up from the lounge chair and motioned for Theo to have a seat.

After only a second's pause, he sat down. "Whose spot am I taking?"

"Sally's," Trish said. "She's at the spa getting a massage."

Theo glanced around looking as ill at ease as Trish felt. "Tell me what you meant."

Think outside the box, she told herself.

"Take off your shirt." For her spur-of-the-moment plan to work, she needed Theo to begin to think like someone on vacation. "Sit back and relax a little."

He looked at her suspiciously.

"None of the men have their shirts on," Trish explained, waving a hand vaguely in the direction of the other chairs. "At least try to look like you're having fun."

Theo glanced around the deck then at her bikini. Slowly he pulled his T-shirt over his head.

Trish did her best not to gawk. After all, she'd been married. She'd seen naked men before. And Theo was hardly naked. But his bare chest was enough to set her heart pounding. She knew the heat flowing through her body had nothing to do with the bright Mediterranean sun and everything to do with the handsome Greek sitting only a few feet away.

He lifted a dark eyebrow, a slight smile playing at

the corners of his lips. "Do I look like I'm having fun now?"

Trish struggled to keep her eyes riveted to Theo's face.

"You're off to a great start," Trish said, adding a teasing lilt to her voice. "But this is just the beginning. The point is not to only *look* like you're having fun, but to actually *have* fun. That's why you need to stay."

Theo tilted his head, his eyes speculative. "Are you offering to teach me?"

"Me?" Trish gave a little laugh. "I'm not qualified. I'm still learning how to have fun myself."

"Ah," he said with an enigmatic smile. "Another novice. Perhaps we could learn together?"

Was it only her imagination or was Theo Catomeris flirting with her? Had she won him over with her brilliant conversational skills or was it her yellow bikini? Actually, she reminded herself, she hadn't won him over, she'd only bought herself a little time.

She still needed to figure out how to make him stay…and then how to make him sign.

CHAPTER EIGHT

"LIE BACK," Trish said in answer. "Close your eyes. Clear your mind and listen to the music."

Her voice softened as she continued to speak, her tone taking on an almost-lyrical quality. Theo supposed he could have gotten up, told her he was too busy for such foolishness. But the truth was he had some free time and he was enjoying her company.

He leaned back and out of the corner of his eye saw her do the same. She had a body made for a bikini…slender curves in all the right places. When she'd called his name and he'd turned, a flash of heat had shot straight to his groin. Which was crazy considering the fact that she was a woman who had been inconsequential…until today.

But that wasn't why he'd followed her. She intrigued him. Which was why he was sitting on this white lounge chair, waiting to see what was going to come out of her mouth.

She was unpredictable. Like when she'd approached the table last night. The conversation had been going smoothly until she'd brought up that blasted contract. He'd be the first to admit that he'd been irritated.

Still, he found himself admiring her tenacity. Though convincing him to do the tours for Liberty was a battle she couldn't possibly win, she kept coming back for more rejection. He had no doubt as to why he was sitting here. She had some scheme in her head.

But the sun was warm, and in spite of his resolve to keep alert, Theo felt himself begin to relax. The music from the band set up by the bar brought back memories of a trip he and his friend Bruno had taken to Fiji their last year in college. His eyes drifted shut, and like a movie in his mind, he found himself reliving the wild adventures they'd had…

"The first cruise I went on was to Hawaii," Trish murmured, pulling him from his thoughts. "They played music very much like this on board. Isn't it funny how sounds can transport you back to another place and time?"

Theo opened his eyes and rolled on his side to face her. "I was just thinking the same thing." He wondered if he'd be out of line to tell her that her eyes were the color of caramels in the light. "Did you go to Hawaii with a friend?"

"No," she said, reaching for the sunscreen bottle, her hair dropping down and blocking her eyes from his view. "I was on my honeymoon."

Theo's smile froze on his lips. He knew she was a Mrs. not a Miss, but he'd noticed she wasn't wearing a ring and had assumed she was divorced. "You have a husband?"

"*Had*," Trish said. "We've been divorced for a long time. Close to five years."

Theo expelled the breath he'd been holding. Of course his relief wasn't because he was interested in her romantically. He just had a policy against socializing with married women. "Any children?"

A brilliant smile flashed across her face. "One. A daughter. Would you like to see her picture?"

"Sure, that—"

She didn't even wait for him to finish before she pulled her bag up to her lap and started rummaging through it. Just as he was about to tell her not to bother, she finally pulled out a little leather case that looked like a man's wallet but contained only pictures. "This is Cassidy at her last birthday party. She's eight."

Theo stared dutifully at the photo. The girl's hair was dark, not red, but her facial features showed a remarkable likeness to her mother. "Cute girl."

Trish ran a finger across the top of the picture and a look of longing filled her gaze. "She's also funny and smart and…"

Theo watched in horror as tears filled her eyes. He felt a ridiculous urge to pat her on the shoulder, or even pull her into his arms and comfort her.

Thankfully he didn't have to act on his impulses. Trish turned away and shoved the small photo album back into her bag. "I'm sorry. I'm not usually so emotional. It's just that this is the first time we've been apart for so long and I find myself missing her terribly."

"I understand," Theo said, although he didn't. He didn't have any children to miss. "I take it she lives with you?"

"Her father and I share custody," Trish said.

His face must have shown his surprise because she smiled. "Coordinating her care can be hard but the arrangement is in Cassidy's best interest. And I'm still the primary custodial parent."

"That must be hard." Theo couldn't imagine how she did it. He knew firsthand the demands of owning a business and the stress she must be under. "Being on your own with a child."

"I guess I don't really feel alone," Trish said, and he was happy to see that all trace of tears had left her eyes. "I have a lot of supportive friends and Steven, my ex-husband, is very involved."

"Is he watching her while you're here?"

"He's out of town on business," Trish said. "She's spending the week with my sister and her family in Disney World."

A sad look crossed her face and for a second he thought she might cry again. Theo shifted uneasily in his seat, wishing he hadn't asked so many questions. After all, he didn't want to care about her daughter or her child-care arrangements. Or how his decision not to sign her contract might affect her personal and business life.

"How about you?" she asked. "Do you have a wife? Kids?"

"No," he said smoothly. "My business doesn't leave me time for much else. I didn't feel it would be fair to have a family come in a distant second."

He didn't know who was more surprised by the last statement, him or her. Normally he just said he was too busy and let it go at that. But over the last few years he'd come to realize his decision to avoid serious relationships went beyond a hectic work schedule.

His mother had spent most of his growing-up years focused on her career, leaving him feeling more like an inconvenience than anything else. He refused to subject a wife or children to that experience.

"Good for you." Trish nodded. "I firmly believe family should come before a career. Unfortunately I've been forced to balance work and home. But I make a conscious effort to put Cassidy's needs first."

"Which means your needs come last?" Theo said.

Trish shrugged. "That's okay. There'll be plenty of time for my needs once she's grown."

Theo couldn't help it. The more she talked, the more he found himself admiring…even liking this woman. She'd not only chosen to devote the best years of her life to focus on her daughter, she did so willingly, even cheerfully.

"So this cruise is a vacation for you."

"I'm here because of business," Trish said pointedly. "I'm here to convince you to sign the contract."

"I already told you no," he said.

Trish lifted her chin. "The party's not over until the fat lady sings."

It was an American colloquialism, but he understood what she was trying to say, and once again he had to admire her determination. Unfortunately, if she remained so focused on this unattainable goal, she wasn't going to be able to enjoy the cruise, which could be her only time for herself for the next few years. Unless...

"Tomorrow we'll be in Naples," Theo said. "Do you have plans?"

Trish looked puzzled. "Why do you ask?"

"I thought I might call up an old friend who lives there to show me the city," Theo said. "And I wondered if you'd like to come along?"

"DID HE SAY ANYTHING more about this friend?" Sally asked, slathering antiaging cream onto her face in front of the bathroom mirror.

Trish thought for a moment. "He said 'old friend' but I don't think it's a grandfather kind of guy. I got the impression he was Theo's age."

A doubtful look crossed Sally's face. "I suppose it will be okay."

Trish resisted the urge to wrap her fingers around Sally's neck. Didn't her friend realize that spending the day with Theo was Trish's dream come true? Now she wouldn't have to scout him out on deck and try to engage him in conversation; she'd have access to him the whole day. Hopefully there would be many, many opportunities to bring up the contract, subtly of course.

"Naples is such a romantic city," Sally said. "I know it may seem like a girlish dream, but I had this vision of you and me sitting in some outdoor eating area, chatting with handsome Italian men."

"We don't speak Italian," Trish reminded her friend even as her heart twisted. Sometimes it was easy to forget that this was Sally's vacation, too.

A dreamy look crossed Sally's face. "Don't they say that the language of love knows no boundaries?"

It was the first time Trish had heard the expression but she got the drift. Sally was a romantic and far be it from Trish to dash her friend's hopes. "Okay, how about this…we go with Theo and meet his friend. If it's not working out, we make some excuse and split?"

Sally added a little extra cream to the barely perceptible lines next to her mouth. "Whatever you want to do is fine with me."

"It's a plan," Trish said, then flipped open her

phone and hit the speed dial for the Orlando hotel. If Cassidy asked her tonight if the man had signed yet, she'd have to say no, but the way it was going she might have some good news to report very, very soon.

THE GARDEN TERRACE on deck eleven was clearly the place to be on this beautiful summer morning. After working out in the fitness center one deck above, Trish had decided to swing by the buffet.

She grabbed a yogurt and a cup of coffee and was headed toward the exit when she spotted Ariana Bennett. The ship's librarian—and fellow American— was seated by herself at a small table by the window.

Though Ariana appeared lost in her own thoughts, Trish decided it would be rude to walk by without saying hello. She got all the way to the table before Ariana looked up.

"Good morning." Trish smiled. "I didn't expect to see you here."

A guilty look skittered across the librarian's face. "I know I shouldn't be eating in a public dining area while I'm on duty but—"

"I didn't mean that," Trish said hurriedly, appalled Ariana thought she could be such a snob. "I just thought you'd be in the library. It seems you're always there."

The tense set of Ariana's shoulders eased. "Once the call to disembark goes out, I'm off duty. I'll be heading off the ship with the passengers."

"I take it no afternoon talks with Father Connelly today?" Though Trish hadn't made any of them so far, she'd heard the informal "chats" in the library had been immensely popular.

Father Patrick Connelly, a priest with vast knowledge of Greek and Roman culture, had been specifically brought on board to share his knowledge with interested passengers. And he used his collection of reproductions of Greek and Roman antiquities, which were displayed in the library, to illustrate his lectures.

Despite the good things Trish had heard about the talks, she didn't plan to attend any. Maybe it was sacrilegious but the man…well, he creeped her out.

She'd run across the middle-aged priest her first day on the ship. Father Connelly had been on the upper deck, ogling the bathing beauties with a decidedly lecherous gleam in his eye.

"No lecture today," Ariana said. "Most of the passengers will be onshore so it didn't make sense to have one."

Trish smiled her agreement, placed her yogurt parfait and spoon on the table and took a sip of her rapidly cooling coffee.

"Oh my goodness," Ariana said. "Where are my manners? Please sit down."

Trish had planned to head straight back to the room but it was early enough that Sally was probably still sleeping. She decided to take Ariana up on her offer. Pulling out a chair, Trish took a seat next to the large window.

"What were we talking about?" Trish asked, sipping her coffee, reveling in the feel of the sun against her cheek.

Ariana made a face. "Father Connelly."

"Everyone says he knows his stuff." Trish chose her words carefully, trying not to let her distaste of the man show.

"He *considers* himself an expert." Ariana's tone made it clear she didn't agree with that assessment. "But he's not always correct. Yesterday, after his lecture, I pulled him aside and gently pointed out a few errors he'd made."

"How'd he take that?" Trish asked.

"Not well." Ariana broke off a piece of Danish and popped it in her mouth. She chewed thoughtfully for a moment. "I probably shouldn't have corrected him, but gosh, the man is so arrogant."

"And a little creepy," Trish added. When she'd seen him looking at those girls on the deck, she'd thought about reporting his behavior to someone. But really, what could she say? That the priest had a decidedly unholy gleam in his eye?

Besides, Trish had more important things on her mind than a rogue priest…

While the ship's journey from Corfu to the Italian

coast had been a smooth one, Trish's dreams had been anything but placid. Thoughts of Theo had invaded her normally G-rated dreams and she'd awakened feeling tense.

That's why she'd hopped out of bed at the crack of dawn, pulled on her workout clothes and headed to the gym. After five hard miles on the treadmill, Trish had felt confident she'd sweated every last errant thought of Theo Catomeris from her system.

"You know who else is creepy?" Trish asked.

"Who?" Ariana leaned forward and rested her elbows on the table.

Trish cast a quick glance at the nearby tables before speaking. "Giorgio Tzekas, the first officer. Do you know which one he is?"

"Our paths have crossed," Ariana said with a wry smile, lifting a cup of coffee to her lips.

"That man thinks he's God's gift to women." Trish remembered the dance they'd shared and the too-tight way he'd held her.

Ariana leaned back. "He's not even that good-looking."

Not like Theo, Trish thought.

"Certainly not as cute as he thinks he is," Trish said.

Ariana started to laugh then quickly sobered. "Speak of the devil."

Trish glanced up just in time to see Giorgio stop beside the table.

"What a pleasant surprise," he said with a slight smile. "Two of my favorite la-dies."

Ariana kicked Trish beneath the table and it took all of Trish's self-control not to laugh.

"You didn't call me last night," Giorgio said in a reproachful tone, his gaze focused on Ariana.

"I never said I would," Ariana replied.

"Apology accepted." Giorgio trailed a finger up Ariana's arm before the librarian jerked it away. "I have the day off. I thought we could explore Naples together."

Trish turned to gaze out the window in an attempt to distance herself from the private conversation.

Her thoughts drifted to Theo. Today she'd apologize and clear the air. Actually, she should have done it before now. It was important he understood that she hadn't known of his relationship with Elias Stamos when she'd first approached him.

"I thought he'd never leave." Ariana heaved an exasperated sigh.

Trish watched Giorgio stride off, his back stiffened in a hard straight line.

"I was trying not to listen." Trish decided that sounded better than admitting she'd been daydreaming. "What bee got in his booty?"

Ariana laughed at one of Cassidy's favorite expressions. "I made it clear I wasn't going to spend the day with him," Ariana said. "Even if I wanted to—which I don't—I have too many—"

She clamped her mouth shut as if she'd already said too much.

As far as Trish was concerned, no explanation was necessary. She couldn't see anyone wanting to waste a bright, sunny day hanging out with Giorgio.

"What are you most interested in seeing?" Trish followed Ariana's example and pushed her chair back and rose to her feet. She understood exactly what Ariana meant. There was so much to see in Naples, even if you went nonstop all day you couldn't cover it all.

"The National Archaeological Museum." Ariana didn't quite meet Trish's gaze. "But I've also got some errands to run. Some specific things I'm looking for…"

Trish wasn't surprised Ariana mentioned the museum. Several of the comments Ariana had made indicated she had an interest in archaeology. "I hope you enjoy the museum," Trish said. "And I hope you find what you're looking for…"

For a second, Ariana's expression grew troubled. "I hope I do, too. Except you know what they say…"

Trish lifted a brow.

"Be careful what you wish for," Ariana said, "because you might just get it."

CHAPTER NINE

"I CAN SEE WHY you like it here." Theo took a sip of beer as her marveled at the brilliant blue of the Bay of Naples. He spoke in Italian, knowing his Italian was better than Bruno's Greek. "This is a great hotel with a fabulous view."

Bruno Tucci leaned back in his chair and smiled as if Theo had complimented his firstborn. "From the moment Sophia and I first saw this place, we knew it was destined to be our home."

Bruno had been Theo's friend during his college years. Back then they'd been as close as brothers and shared many adventures. But once Bruno met Sophia his senior year, the partying and staying out late with friends had come to an abrupt halt. After graduating from the University of Athens, Bruno had returned to Italy, bought a hotel, married Sophia and had a couple of kids. Two years ago his wife had died in a car accident. Theo hadn't been back to Italy since the funeral.

The luxury hotel that Bruno owned and managed

was on the side of Posillipo Hill overlooking the city of Naples. Though Theo had made plans with Trish, when he'd heard her friend wanted to sleep in, they arranged to meet later at the hotel. Theo had arrived early and spent the morning getting reacquainted with his goddaughters—five-year-old Anna and seven-year-old Isabella.

Before Bruno's girls headed over to a neighbor's house to play for the day, they'd each given their father a huge hug and a kiss.

Theo had watched in silence, thinking of Trish. It must have been hard for her to leave her daughter behind.

After the girls had gone, Theo and Bruno re-hashed old times.

"Sophia always loved the view from here," Bruno said, mentioning his beloved wife.

Ten years ago, Theo had been the best man at Bruno's wedding. Once his friend had met spunky and beautiful Sophia, he'd never looked at another woman.

"Think you'll marry again?" Theo asked.

"Definitely," Bruno said, without even stopping to think. "I liked being married. Unfortunately the children and hotel keep me so busy, there's little time to date. How about you?"

"Business is good," Theo said. "I'm juggling some figures now to see if I can afford another boat. And, of course, my foundation for the horses of Kefalonia keeps me busy."

"I was talking about marriage," Bruno said. "You love children and you're good with them. Surely you want a wife and family of your own…"

Theo took a sip of beer and kept his tone casual. "I'm forty years old, my friend. I'm past all that."

Bruno snorted. "We're in the prime of our lives."

Theo laughed at Bruno's indignant tone. "Maybe so."

Bruno took a sip of wine. "You just haven't met the one yet."

"The one?"

"The one who sets your blood on fire," Bruno said. "The one who nourishes your soul. The one you cannot live without."

"It appears," Theo said with a smile, "that you have turned into a poet."

"Theo," Bruno chided, "all I'm asking is that you be open if such a person should stumble into your life."

"I'll be open," Theo hedged, more to forestall more badgering than out of any real agreement. "After all, I'm an open-minded man. Didn't I agree to meet my half sisters?"

"I'm proud of you for that." Bruno leaned forward, his handsome face serious. "Katherine and Helena are your family. It's good you get to know them.

Tommy and Menka aren't getting any younger. Once your grandparents are gone, you'll be all alone."

It was a sobering thought and Theo would be lying if he said it had never crossed his mind. "You're forgetting about my mother."

A look of distaste crossed Bruno's face. "How is Tasia?"

Bruno's tone made it clear there was no love lost between him and the woman who'd given birth to Theo. Ever since Anastasia had tried to seduce Bruno his freshman year in college, Bruno had wanted nothing to do with the woman.

For all his worldly ways and Italian charm, Bruno had very traditional values. Sleeping with his best friend's mother—no matter how beautiful the woman—wasn't something he'd ever contemplate.

"I don't speak with her much," Theo said. "Although I'll probably call her tonight. She knew I was meeting Katherine and Helena, so she'll be expecting an update."

"What are you going to tell her?" Bruno asked, signaling the waiter to bring another round of drinks.

Theo grinned. "As little as possible."

Bruno clapped him on the shoulder. "Smart man."

High-pitched voices and laughter sounded from the entryway. Bruno lifted a questioning brow.

"Looks like the Americans have arrived," Theo said. Thankfully when Theo had told Bruno he'd asked two women he'd met on the ship to join them, Bruno had been all for it.

"My God, she is absolutely stunning," Bruno said, looking at Trish.

Theo's fingers tightened around his glass of beer. His friend was right…she *was* stunning. Even in a simple sleeveless dress with her hair pulled back from her face, she had a beauty that took his breath away.

"I never knew you liked redheads," Theo said, hating the jealousy rising in him.

"Redhead?" Bruno threw back his head and laughed as if Theo had said something uproariously funny. "I'm talking about the blonde."

Theo didn't know whether to be insulted on Trish's behalf or relieved that his handsome friend wasn't going to make a move on her.

"The blonde's name is Sally," Theo said.

"Perfect." Bruno pushed back his chair and stood, reverting to English. "Ladies, welcome."

The blond woman responded immediately. Her red lips parted and her baby-blue eyes widened.

Theo had never paid much attention to Sally. A little taller and slightly heavier than Trish, the woman had curves in all the right places and an exceedingly pretty face. He could see why she'd caught Bruno's eye.

The funny thing was, her beauty left Theo cold. But then, he'd always been partial to redheads.

Since when, a tiny little voice in his head jeered. Theo ignored it. Granted, he hadn't run across many redheads, but he found the hair color strikingly different.

Theo rose to his feet and reminded himself that he'd only invited Trish so that she could enjoy the day without feeling guilty. And if he was happy to see her it was only because he couldn't wait to see how she would try to interject the business into the day's pleasure.

"YOU NEVER TOLD ME Theo's friend was gorgeous." Sally spoke out of the corner of her mouth, keeping her smile firmly in place.

"I had no idea what he looked like," Trish said. Though Bruno was definitely attractive, he couldn't begin to compare to Theo.

Trish shoved the realization aside. The last thing she wanted was to think of Theo in *that* way. Today was about business, interspersed with a little sightseeing. Nothing more.

With that thought firmly fixed in her mind, Trish crossed the room to where Theo and Bruno stood. But when she stepped out onto the patio, the view of Naples forced every other thought from her head. Even the slight haze hovering over the city couldn't detract from the breathtaking picture.

"This would be a great excursion stop," Trish

said. "A place for some light refreshments, a perfect photo-op."

"Trish arranges tour excursions for cruise ships," Theo said, making quick work of the introductions.

Though Bruno kept slanting glances in Sally's direction, he focused his attention on Trish. "I would be much interested in having your excursions stop here."

Trish slipped open her purse and pulled out a card. Although her primary focus was getting Theo to sign, she wasn't about to pass up another business opportunity. "I'll be back in the States next week. Give me a call and we'll see what we can work out."

Bruno took the card and glanced at it before putting it in his pocket. "*Grazie*, Signora Melrose."

"I love your hotel." Sally placed her hand on Bruno's arm, drawing his attention back to her.

"Please have a seat." Bruno pulled out a chair for Sally with a flourish.

It would be so easy to fall in love in this country, Trish thought with a sigh. The men oozed charm and the beautiful scenery only added to the romantic ambience.

Bruno glanced momentarily at Theo. Trish wasn't sure what the look meant until Theo said, "The hotel has some beautiful gardens. I'd like to show you my favorite."

Now Trish understood. Bruno's message was clear: "Do something, I want to be alone with Sally."

Trish slanted a sideways glance at her friend. The gleam in Sally's eyes told her Sally was as eager to get rid of her as Bruno was to get rid of Theo.

"A walk would be nice," Trish agreed.

Theo rested his hand on her back, guiding her across the outdoor dining area to a stone pathway. They'd only walked about ten feet when they came to a set of steps made out of rock. When she stepped forward, Theo's hand closed around her arm.

"These are steep," he warned.

"Not for the faint of heart," Trish said, taking each step carefully. The sun warmed her and the sweet scent of flowers filled the air. A hint of a breeze caressed her cheek.

"This is a perfect day," Trish said finally, when they both stood at the bottom of the steps.

He gazed at her for a long moment. "Your hair looks very red in the light."

Trish gave a little laugh. "Gee, thanks."

"I meant it as a compliment," Theo said. "I like the coppery color…especially on you."

There was something different about Theo today, Trish decided. He seemed less stressed, more like a person on vacation. This was the opportunity she'd been hoping for, a chance to explain and ask for forgiveness.

"There's something I need to say." Trish turned and faced Theo.

His shoulders tensed. "If it's about the contract—"

"It is—"

"I'm not changing—"

"I want to apologize."

"—my mind." Theo paused. "What did you say?"

Trish clasped her hands together to still their trembling. Who knew two little words could be so difficult?

"I'm sorry," Trish said. "I didn't know that Elias Stamos was your father the other last night. Or that this whole contract thing was part of some family disagreement. Believe me, if I *had* known I'd have refused to ask, no matter what it cost me. I—"

Theo was frowning.

"Okay, maybe I still would have asked," Trish said, a tiny smile quirking her lips. "But I would have approached it from a different angle."

"He threatened you?"

Trish was startled. "Threatened?"

Theo studied her closely. "You said it would have cost you."

Trish hesitated, but she knew she was only delaying the inevitable. Theo wasn't going to accept her apology without an explanation. "Stamos made noises like he might cancel my company contracts if you didn't sign," she said quickly, the words tumbling out. "But I'm sure he'd have reconsidered. Holding me accountable for a decision that wasn't mine to make would hardly be fair."

Even to her ears Trish didn't sound very convincing, but she knew she'd only make it worse if she said more.

"It wouldn't be fair," Theo murmured, almost to himself. He shook his head before his clear-eyed gaze met hers. "Apology accepted."

"Okay, then." Trish expelled the breath she didn't realize she'd been holding. Impulsively she stuck out her hand. "Friends?"

For a second he looked taken aback, but his hand closed over hers. "Friends."

He didn't immediately pull away as she'd expected, and instant heat pulsed through her, followed quickly by goose bumps over her skin. But before she could do something incredibly foolish and risk the tentative friendship they'd just forged, Trish slid her hand from his. "How far is it to the garden?"

She could feel Theo's eyes on her but she refused to look his way. "Around the next bend."

He resumed walking and she fell into step beside him. When he slowed to a stop in front of the garden, Trish's breath caught in her throat.

An explosion of color assaulted her senses. Flowers of every shape and size were in full bloom and she realized that the seductively sweet scent that had teased her nostrils earlier had come from this beautiful area.

Impulsively she leaned over and fingered the silky petals of a purple flower. "It's like the Garden of Eden."

"Bruno's wife designed it," Theo said.

Trish stilled then slowly straightened. "Bruno is married?"

Hot anger twisted her stomach into a knot. She'd heard Italian men were notorious womanizers. But she couldn't believe the man had the audacity to flirt so shamelessly with Sally…with his staff watching…under the same roof as his wife. And Theo had known…

"How could you not tell me? Your friend has a *wife*." Her voice trembled with barely restrained fury. "Yet he's in the dining room right now flirting with Sally. You call that acceptable behavior?"

Her voice had risen and turned shrill but Trish didn't care. If she had a hot button, it was infidelity.

"Bruno's wife is dead," Theo said quietly. "Sophia died in a car accident two years ago."

"I'm sorry," Trish said, feeling like a fool…again. "I shouldn't have jumped to conclusions."

"I understand wanting to protect a friend."

"It's not just that," Trish said. "In my mind someone who cheats is the lowest of the low."

Theo stared at her for a long moment. "He cheated on you."

"What?"

"Your ex-husband," Theo said, his eyes dark and watchful. "He was unfaithful."

Trish raised a hand. "I don't really want to—" she began then stopped herself. Why was she covering for Steven? "Yes, he cheated on me."

Theo stepped forward and tipped her chin up with his finger. "He was a fool."

For a long moment her eyes locked with his. The air grew thick and the chirping birds and buzz of bees faded into nothingness. A strange electricity filled the air and Trish began to wonder if you really could drown in someone's eyes.

When his head began to lower, Trish held her breath. She didn't know if what she was about to do was a smart thing or not. She only knew she couldn't move, didn't want to move.

His lips were mere inches away when his cell phone rang. It wasn't a song like the ring tone she used, but a shrill, irritating sound that demanded attention.

Theo jerked back and Trish swallowed a cry of disappointment.

Pressing his lips together, Theo flipped open the phone. When he spoke it was in Italian, and Trish could only understand every third or fourth word.

Theo snapped the phone shut. "It was Bruno. They want us back at the hotel to discuss some important plans."

"We'd better go then," Trish said with a bright

smile. She didn't give Theo a chance to say anything, she just turned and headed for the stairs, telling herself she should be grateful the call had come when it did. The trouble was she didn't feel grateful.

Theo cupped her elbow with his hand when she paused at the bottom of the steps.

Trish climbed the steep incline, knowing her unsteadiness had far more to do with Theo's touch than wobbly shoes on narrow steps. Only with Herculean effort did she manage to cover the last few feet to the back patio without collapsing into a mass of quivering jelly.

Sally was waiting when she got to the outdoor dining area. "Bruno has the motorbikes all ready. Where have you two been?"

"Motorcycles?" Trish took a step back, bumping into Theo. Her father had been seriously injured on a motorcycle when she was a small girl. Trish still remembered going up to the hospital to see him. "I'm not getting on one."

"These are not motorcycles," Bruno said. "They're Vespa motorbikes, scooters."

"I don't care," Trish insisted. "Count me out."

"C'mon, Trish," Sally said. "It'll be fun."

Trish crossed her arms over her chest. "You remember how long it took my father to recover from that accident. I'm not doing it, Sally. End of story."

Trish saw Theo and Bruno exchange glances.

"Trish, I really want to do this," Sally said, not giving up. "Bruno says there are some great places we can explore on the bikes."

"I didn't say that *you* can't go. I'm just not going to do it myself."

"I have an idea," Theo said. "How about if Trish and I take the rental car and check out the street market while you and Sally take the motorbikes for a spin. We can meet up back at the dock."

"No," Trish objected. "You go with your friend. He's the one you came to see. Please, don't spoil your fun because of me."

Theo took her hand and brought it to his lips. "I spent the morning with Bruno. I want to spend the rest of the day with you."

"If you're sure…" Trish said.

"I've never been more sure of anything in my life."

CHAPTER TEN

"Greeks founded the city of Naples in the seventh century, B.C." Theo whipped the tiny Smart car into a miniscule parking place on the city street, relieved it fit into the small space with room to spare. "In fact the ancient design of the city still exists and can be seen today."

Back in the garden, he'd almost let the moment override his good sense. Though he hadn't appreciated the interruption at the time, he was now glad Bruno had called. He'd wanted to show Trish a good time today, and kissing her could have ruined the fragile truce between them.

"Three long parallel streets cross the center of Naples, with a series of small, narrow streets connecting them." Theo pulled the key from the ignition, dropped it into his pocket and reached for the door handle. "Wait. I'll open the door for you."

"I can do—"

But Theo was out of the car and around it before she had a chance to finish. His grandmother had taught him from a young age what it meant to be a gentleman.

"Thank you, Theo." Trish took his hand and stepped out of the car. Once on the sidewalk she turned completely around, taking it all in. "So many people in such a small area."

"Space is at a premium." The narrow street was crowded with vendors selling everything from shoes to fresh fruit and flowers.

"I'm glad you suggested coming here," Trish said, excitement in her voice.

He gestured toward the vendors lining the streets. "Shall we check them out?"

But Trish hesitated. "Are you sure Gladys is going to be okay?"

Theo couldn't help but chuckle at the name she'd given the car on the short drive down the hill. "Gladys will be fine."

"If Sally and Bruno hadn't decided to meet us at the dock, we would have had to call a cab to take us back to the ship." Trish glanced at the bright red vehicle. "The three of us would never have fit in her."

"We would have figured out something," Theo began.

"Look," Trish exclaimed, pulling him forward. "Shopping carts full of shoes."

Though metal carts filled with leather loafers had never held much appeal, Theo found her enthusiasm contagious. "Just remember," he teased, "Gladys can't hold more than a few dozen pairs."

"Ha, ha," she said, before turning her attention to the shoes. But then, as if realizing she'd forgotten something, she reached out and grabbed Theo's hand, pulling him to her side. "Help me look. I wear size thirty-six."

She looked so beautiful with the sun shining down on her coppery hair. An unexpected warmth rose up inside him and Theo decided shopping for shoes might not be quite so boring after all.

He'd just picked up a pair of sandals when his phone rang. It was a standard tone, very similar to the one that had announced Bruno's call. He recognized it immediately and it was all he could do not to groan.

"Aren't you going to answer?" Trish asked. "It could be Bruno."

He could have explained that it was his mother, the last person he wanted to converse with on a beautiful summer day. But that would lead to questions. It seemed simpler to just answer the call. Theo flipped open the phone and switched to Greek. "Hello, Mother."

"Theo, what's that noise in the background? Where are you?"

"Naples," he said. "At the street market."

"In Naples?" Her voice rose. "What are you doing in Italy?"

His mother had been known to go months without talking to him. But once she'd learned Katherine Stamos had contacted him, Tasia had suddenly become interested in his every move.

"I'm visiting Bruno," Theo said, picking a reason that wouldn't prompt too many questions. "You remember Bruno Tucci, my friend from college."

"Of course," Tasia said smoothly. "Give him my regards."

"I'll do that." Theo paused and waited for her to get to the real reason she'd called.

"You were supposed to phone me after your meeting with those women," she said. "I haven't heard from you."

The edge was back in her voice, the same edge that was there whenever Elias Stamos or his family was mentioned.

Her bitterness toward Elias and his family had been a part of her for as long as Theo could remember. He knew the last thing she'd want to hear was that the meeting had gone well.

"It went," Theo said flatly, conscious of Trish's curious gaze.

"What did you think of them?" his mother pressed. "Do you plan to see them again?"

"I suppose our paths will cross sometime in the future. I'm not sure when."

That was true, as far as it went. He wasn't *exactly*

sure when they'd be getting together. Dinner with Helena tonight had been discussed but not finalized.

"That family is nothing but trouble," Tasia said. "Mark my words—"

"Look, Mother, I need to go." Theo refused to waste one more minute of this beautiful afternoon hearing her berate the Stamos family. He'd heard it all before. "Ciao."

"Anything wrong?"

Theo turned to find Trish staring, a pair of conservative leather loafers in one hand.

"Not at all." He frowned. "You're going to buy those?"

"You don't like them?" She turned the shoes over in her hand, reinspecting them. "They're a bargain."

"They just don't seem like your type of shoes. Too plain."

"I think you're being presumptuous."

"How so?"

"You have this image of me in your head," she said. "And I'm not sure it's entirely accurate."

Actually she was wrong. He didn't have an image of her fixed in his mind at all. But the more time he spent with her, the more he felt he was getting to know her.

The noise around them dimmed as Trish looked up at him. The only thing he was conscious of was the plump juicy redness of her lips.

"*Signorina,* you like the shoes?" the vendor asked.

Trish blinked and turned to the man. "What?"

"You like the shoes?" The beady-eyed man asked again. "I make you good deal."

Theo shot the man a black look but he simply smiled and looked at Trish with a hopeful expression.

"I'm not sure," Trish said. "I think I'll look a little more before I decide." She placed the shoes back on the cart and grabbed Theo's hand. "Let's explore."

They'd barely gone five feet when Trish abruptly stopped. "Ariana."

The librarian whirled, her eyes wide. "Trish. What are you doing here?"

"Shopping." Trish laughed. "Just like the majority of the passengers who came onshore."

"Of course," Ariana said, but Theo noticed the woman's smile looked strained, and she turned her back on the vendor she'd been speaking with only moments before.

Trish, however, seemed oblivious to Ariana's discomfort. She glanced over the librarian's shoulder and her eyes widened at the statuary on display. "Wow. He's got some nice stuff."

"It's okay," Ariana said. "Nothing spectacular."

"It's amazing how real these reproductions can look. If I—"

"We don't have much time left," Ariana said. "I'm

surprised you don't have a shopping bag already filled with treasures."

"You're right," Trish agreed. "We should get going. So much to see and do and so little time."

Something that looked a lot like relief filled the woman's eyes. While Theo had the feeling Ariana was happy to see them go, he knew she couldn't be as happy as he was…to be alone with Trish once again.

"NOTHING SPECTACULAR?" The antiquities vendor raised a brow.

"They were from the ship," Ariana said in a clipped tone. "I wanted them gone. If I'd raved about your inventory she'd still be here."

"Not if the man had his way. There was more on his mind than shopping." The vendor chuckled and made some lurid gestures with his fingers.

It was all Ariana could do not to snap at him. Time *was* racing by and the man was behaving like a blasted adolescent.

"I didn't come halfway across the world to talk about them," she said, forcing a conciliatory tone. "What I need to know is, can you get the piece or not?"

"I'm sorry, *signorina*," the man said, not appearing at all sorry. "Even if I could locate that piece for you, you would not be able to take such an item from the country."

Another closed door. But she wasn't about to let

him pat her on the head and send her on her way. There was too much at stake. In order to prove her father wasn't guilty of antiquities theft and restore his good name, Ariana had to investigate all leads.

Leads like dealers who'd been listed as contacts in her father's notebook. From them she hoped to find out who her father had dealt with at various archaeological sites.

"Look." Ariana planted both hands on the table and leaned forward. "Does the name Derek Bennett mean anything to you?"

He rubbed his chin, his gaze thoughtful. But the momentary flicker in his eyes told Ariana she'd hit pay dirt.

She held her breath.

"There's a dig in Paestum, not far from here," he said finally. "When you get to the site, ask for Nico. Tell him I sent you. He'll get you what you want."

Ariana's head was spinning. After all her searching, she was finally getting somewhere. She cleared her throat. "Does this Nico have a last name?"

The man was silent a moment. "Nico is enough."

Ariana pulled a tiny notebook and pen from her pocket and wrote the name down, though there was no way she would forget it. "And you said the dig is in Paestum?"

The man nodded.

Ariana glanced at her watch. It was already three.

She had to be back on board by five. That still gave her a good two hours. "Is it close?"

"Not too far," the man said. "About a hundred kilometers from here."

Ariana mentally converted kilometers to miles and her heart sank. There was no way she could go sixty miles there and back before the ship sailed. "Does Nico work every day?"

The man nodded, making a shooing gesture. "I'm here to sell, not talk."

Ariana shoved the paper with the contact information into her purse. "Thank you for your help."

Only after the words had left her lips did Ariana discover she'd wasted her breath. The man had already turned away to talk to a real customer. She didn't care. She had what she wanted; a name, a contact.

She glanced at her watch again, hoping she'd read it wrong…finding out she hadn't. No matter how much she wanted to go to Paestum this afternoon, there simply wasn't time.

There will be other days, she told herself. Other days to talk to Nico. Other days to prove that her father *had* been the Knight-in-Shining-Armor of her youth.

Ariana's fingers tightened around her bag, remembering those horrible days following her father's arrest. The prosecutor in the case had been confident he'd get a conviction. Her father had maintained his innocence, and Ariana and her mother had given him their full support.

Unfortunately Derek Bennett had died of a heart attack before he could clear his name. The case had been closed with everyone thinking her father was a crook. That's why Ariana had resigned her job back in Pennsylvania and joined the cruise ship. The police hadn't found her father's notebook with all his contacts listed. Derek had been a curator in a museum and Ariana planned to seek out those contacts and try to clear his name.

Her father was innocent, and as soon as she could get to Paestum, she would start gathering evidence to prove it.

The vendor watched until Ariana was out of sight, then dialed a familiar number. "She came by. It was as I thought."

"Was she satisfied with your answers?"

"She's tenacious, this one," the vendor said. "Talk, talk, talk. I finally told her to go to the site in Paestum and ask for Nico."

"You sent her here?"

The vendor heard the displeasure in the man's voice and his palms began to sweat. "Relax. I didn't tell her anything. And now that you know she's coming, you can be prepared."

"Oh, we'll be prepared all right." The voice took on a deadly calm. "We know how to handle a woman who asks too many questions and sticks her nose where it doesn't belong."

The vendor clicked off the phone, almost feeling sorry for Ariana Bennett. But the man was right about one thing. The woman had stuck her nose where it didn't belong. And she was just about to learn how dangerous that could be.

CHAPTER ELEVEN

TRISH HAD JUST GOTTEN OFF the phone with Cassidy and was refreshing her makeup when Sally came waltzing into the cabin, humming a popular love song.

"Someone is in a good mood," Trish said, flashing her roommate a welcoming smile.

"Someone is in a *great* mood," Sally corrected.

"For a second I wondered if you were going to make it back on the ship at all." Trish kept her tone light. She was, after all, merely Sally's roommate, not her mother. But she had been worried.

Trish and Theo had waited at the dock for Sally and Bruno for the longest time. She'd tried Sally's cell but had been unable to reach her. With no Sally in sight, and the time for reboarding the ship ticking down, Trish had decided there had been a mix-up and that Sally was already on board. But when she'd arrived at their cabin and there had been no sign of her friend, her worry meter had started clanging.

"Bruno is very responsible." Sally sighed. "Sometimes too responsible."

Trish sensed there was more to that comment but she didn't ask. Knowing Sally, she'd soon have all the answers.

"Theo and I went to the street market in Naples," Trish said, dusting her face with powder. "You would have loved it. They were selling anything and everything."

"Sounds like you had fun, too."

Trish paused for a moment and reflected on the afternoon. "I had a very nice time. But I'm kicking myself now. I didn't bring up the contract. Not once in all those hours we were together. What was I thinking?"

"You probably didn't want to ruin the day," Sally replied in a matter-of-fact tone. "Anyway, everything doesn't have to be business."

Trish understood what Sally was saying but she still felt guilty. Twyla and James were counting on her. She couldn't help but feel she'd let them down. "I just wish I'd mentioned—"

"Did he kiss you?" Sally asked abruptly.

Trish dropped her container of loose powder on the counter with a clatter, remembering the incident in the garden. "No."

"Why did you say it that way?" Sally looked puzzled. "Don't you like him?"

"Of course I like him," Trish said honestly. "He's a very nice man. But you have to remember that whatever is between us is strictly business. And that's the way it needs to stay."

Now *that*, Trish knew, wasn't entirely accurate, but it was as good an excuse as any. The truth of the matter was, Theo hadn't kissed her yet. He'd had several good opportunities, and a couple of times she felt sure it was going to happen…then…nothing.

Sally opened her mouth as if to argue, then must have decided against it.

"Enough about me," Trish said, uncapping a tube of lipstick. "How was your afternoon? What did you and Bruno do?"

Sally kicked off her shoes and flopped back on the bed, a big smile on her lips. "Rode motorbikes. Saw the countryside. Kissed a little."

The lipstick Trish had been applying took a detour across her cheek. "You did not."

Sally sat up, resting on her elbows. "You knew we were going to ride the motorbikes."

"You kissed him?" Trish scrubbed her cheek with a tissue, ignoring the niggling thought that if she'd had the chance she'd have done the same thing.

"It was so romantic." Sally's eyes turned dark and dreamy. "We stopped at this grove of olive trees. The sun was shining. Bruno put his arm around me, explaining the difference between black and green olives and…well…suddenly we were kissing."

"That does sound romantic," Trish admitted, ignoring a brief stab of jealousy.

"I like him, Trish," Sally said. "We had so much fun."

Trish's heart softened at the barely perceptible quiver in her friend's voice and the vulnerability in her eyes.

"He lives in Italy," Trish said reminded her gently.

"He wants to see me again."

"I'm sure he does," Trish said. "You're a wonderful woman. The problem is we're only going to be in this part of the world for a few more days."

The minute the words left her mouth Trish wished she could pull them back. All they did was remind her how little time there was to convince Theo to sign and how she'd squandered a whole day of opportunities. Heck, she could have at least mentioned the horses…

But starting tonight she was going to remedy that situation. No more having fun. It was time to get back to business.

THE DINING ROOM had started to thin out, but a few tables still had passengers finishing up dessert or enjoying an after-dinner cappuccino.

"If you have time, stop by the casino." The man sitting next to Sally stood, but his gaze lingered on her. "I should be at the blackjack table most of the night."

Trish watched in amazement as Sally flashed the man a noncommittal smile and immediately refocused her attention on her bowl of strawberries.

"Are you not feeling well?" Trish asked. Rod, a divorced dentist from Iowa, had been flirting with Sally all night, but her friend had been uncharacteristically silent.

Sally looked up in surprise. "I feel fine. Why do you ask?"

"Well, for starters," Trish said, "you were super quiet while we were eating. And now you blow off the guy you've spent the past couple of nights trying to impress."

Sally took a sip of coffee before answering. "I've decided he's not my type."

"When did you decide this?"

"Today."

Ah yes, Trish thought, now Sally's behavior made sense. "After you kissed Bruno."

Trish didn't make it a question because there was no doubt in her mind. And she didn't bother to hide her disapproval. Couldn't Sally see that she was just setting herself up for heartbreak?

"What is your problem?" Sally fixed Trish with a firm look. "I kissed the guy. I didn't tear off my clothes and spread my legs."

Out of the corner of her eye Trish saw the honeymoon couple sitting across the table abruptly stop their conversation, apparently deciding what Sally had to say was more interesting.

"Come with me." Trish pushed back her chair and rose to her feet. "I want to show you a statue in the library. I saw one exactly like it when I was shopping in Naples."

Sally dropped her napkin on the table and stood. "Since when have you been into antiques?"

Trish cast a pointed glance in the direction of the honeymooners and lowered her voice to a barely audible whisper. "Since they quit talking to listen."

Sally chuckled and followed Trish past a group of waiters clearing a nearby table. Partially hidden from view by the servers, Trish couldn't resist glancing at Theo, who was having dinner with his sister.

Dressed in a charcoal shirt and gray tie, he could have been a model on the cover of a men's magazine. But no model had the power to make her heart beat fast and her knees grow weak. And not one of them, she reminded herself, had the power to negatively impact her business.

Trish had seen Theo enter the dining room earlier but she'd deliberately tried not to glance in his direction, wanting to give him his space.

"Look, there's Theo." Sally's loud pronouncement jerked Trish from her reverie. "Let's say hello."

Without waiting for Trish to respond, Sally turned

and headed straight toward Theo. Trish found herself trailing after her impulsive friend.

Theo rose to his feet as they approached. His smile was warm and Trish's heart skipped a beat.

Sally flashed her own smile. "We thought we'd stop by and say hi."

"I'm happy you did." Theo made brief work of introducing Sally to his sister, then turned to Trish. "Would you care to join us? We're just about to order dessert."

His invitation sounded sincere but Trish assumed the offer was a polite gesture, nothing more. "I'm afraid we have other plans."

Theo didn't bat an eye at the refusal or inquire into their plans. Instead he focused his attention on Sally. "I hear you and Bruno had a good time this afternoon."

Sally's face brightened. "You talked to him?"

"He called me after he dropped you off," Theo said. "He couldn't stop talking about you. I haven't seen him this happy in a long time."

"He's a great guy," Sally said, blushing like a schoolgirl.

"Did you enjoy your time in Naples?" Helena asked Trish.

"Very much," Trish said. "I even discovered a lovely hotel that might work out as a future excursion stop."

"Smart woman," Helena remarked with obvious

approval. "It's always good when you can combine business with pleasure."

Trish almost winced, but managed a weak smile.

Helena was now openly staring at Theo, obviously expecting him to pick up the conversational ball. But he didn't and, when an awkward silence descended, Trish decided she'd lingered long enough. "It was nice seeing you again. Enjoy your dessert."

By the time she exited the dining room, she was heartsick. "I blew it," she muttered. "I should have mentioned that contract today when I had the chance. Who knows if I'll have another opportunity."

Sally ignored Trish and started up the steps. For a second Trish couldn't figure out where they were going. Then she realized it had to be the library, the ruse she'd used to get Sally to leave the dining room.

They quickly reached Deck 6 and Sally slowed her pace as they passed Temptations, the chocolate café, but she didn't even glance at the morsels displayed.

"I'm happy you enjoyed yourself today," Trish said. "I really am. Even though you just had a day with the guy, you made the most of it."

"About that…"

The little hitch in her friend's voice gave Trish pause.

"There's something I haven't told you." Sally's words came out in a rush. "When we dock in Livorno, Bruno is going to be there waiting for me. His girls will be spending the week with his sister in

Florence. After Bruno drops them off, he's going to swing by and pick me up."

Trish's head spun and she wasn't sure what to ask first. "His girls?"

"Anna and Isabella," Sally said. "They're five and seven. Bruno and I stopped back at the hotel before we left for the ship and I had the chance to meet them. They're darling girls, Trish. Cassidy would love them."

Trish put a hand to her head but the confusion remained and other questions arose. "What about our trip to see the Leaning Tower of Pisa?"

"I realize it's not fair to bail on you at this late date." Sally sounded genuinely apologetic. "But when Bruno asked me to spend the rest of the week with him, I thought you and Theo would be together."

"The rest of the week?" Trish's voice came out a high-pitched squeak. "You're not coming back to the ship at all?"

"I thought we'd meet up when the ship docks in Barcelona," Sally said.

"But—"

"Ladies, haven't you heard?" A female voice with a Southern accent broke into the conversation. "The library is closed for the evening."

A forty-something blonde with big hair stared pointedly at Trish's hand, now wrapped loosely around the library doorknob.

"The librarian fell on the gangway when she was returning to the ship," the woman continued in a chatty tone usually reserved for old friends. "I heard she sprained her ankle pretty bad and is laid up in the infirmary."

Despite her own pressing concerns, Trish's heart went out to Ariana. What rotten luck. She had been so excited to go ashore and now would probably be confined to the ship for the duration of the cruise.

"I bet they assign another crew member to fill in for her." The woman's eyes brightened. "I hope it's that darling Father Connelly."

It took everything Trish had not to roll her eyes at the mention of the priest. Thankfully someone called to the woman from down the hall and she hurried off.

"Where were we?" Trish asked.

"You were about to tell me how stupid it would be for me to go off with Bruno," Sally said with a rueful smile.

"You barely know the guy, Sal." Trish hated to be so predictably practical but she felt she had to say *something*.

"He's a good guy, Trish." Sally grabbed Trish's arm and pulled her over to a couple of chairs. "And he's not out for what he can get, though I think he'd take it if it were offered."

Something in the way her friend said the words made Trish laugh.

"I feel this connection with Bruno and I'd really like a chance to get to know him better." Sally leaned forward, resting her elbows on her knees. "If there is something between us, we might even stay in touch when I get back to the States."

"But to go off with a man you don't even know…I worry about that."

"He and Theo have been friends for a long time," Sally said. "And I do know him. At least a little. We have so much in common, it's unreal. Do you know he loves opera and gourmet cooking? And we're both crazy about soccer—except he calls it football."

"That's great, Sal, really great," Trish said, not sure what else to say.

"I know it sounds clichéd, but I never expected to meet someone like him."

Trish pushed down the envy that rose up inside her. She understood exactly what Sally was saying.

"Go. Have fun." Trish smiled. "If you're asking for my blessing, you have it."

"Are you sure?" Sally reached over and took Trish's hands. "Because I don't want to leave you in the lurch."

As much as she wanted a friend to pal around with, Trish had meant what she'd said. Sally deserved this chance for happiness. And in a way her friend's departure might be a hidden blessing.

Trish only had thirty-six hours left to convince Theo to sign, and she had the feeling that task was going to take every minute and all her attention.

CHAPTER TWELVE

AGAINST HIS BETTER judgment, Theo watched Trish walk out of the dining room and disappear from view. He'd done his best not to glance in her direction while she was eating, but when she'd come over to the table he hadn't been able to keep his eyes off her.

She looked simply delectable, like a key lime sorbet. The light green dress wrapped itself around her body, emphasizing her curves. She'd done something different with her hair, twisting it in some kind of stylish knot.

"Carpe diem," Helena said, raising a glass of wine to her lips, gold bracelets jangling on her wrist.

Theo shifted his attention back to his sister. "What did you say?"

"Seize the day. It's time you made your move."

"What are you talking about?" Theo asked.

"I saw how you looked at her," Helena said.

"Trish Melrose is an attractive woman. But acting on that attraction is another matter."

Helena tilted her head and he groaned inwardly. It

appeared his response had piqued her interest. "What's wrong with her? She seems like a nice woman."

Theo had thought his reasons would be obvious but it looked as though he was going to have to spell them out. "Her ties with your father for one thing."

"I thought you already settled that issue." Helena took a sip of wine.

"She's still hoping I'll sign."

Helena waved that objection aside, her expression thoughtful. She tapped one long, perfectly manicured nail on the table. "Tell me what's really holding you back."

Her gaze remained firmly fixed on him, and Theo decided if this was what it was like to have a sister, growing up as an only child had been a good thing after all.

"There can never be anything between us," Theo said. "So what's the point?"

Helena burst into laughter. "Who cares? You're in the Mediterranean, one of the most beautiful areas on earth. *Alexandra's Dream* is one of the finest cruise ships in the world. And the penthouse has a terrific Jacuzzi. You've got mood and location, all you need is the woman."

Theo frowned. "I don't use women."

"What if all she wants is a quick fling?" Helena insisted.

What if I want more? Theo suppressed the words

before they made it to his lips. When he'd been in his twenties, a quick fling under the Mediterranean sun would have been just what he was looking for…but he was older now.

"You really think she'd go for that?" Thankfully his words came out without any telling emotion.

"Odds are good. After all, this is the twenty-first century. Not all women want a ring on their finger or something permanent. Sometimes girls just want to have fun."

While sex for the sake of sex still held a certain appeal—especially considering the way Trish made him feel—Theo wasn't sure he wouldn't end up wanting more. And that could be disastrous.

"Or you could just be friends," Helena suggested.

Theo pondered Helena's words. *Friends*. He might be able to handle that. He enjoyed Trish's company and, as her friend, he could show her the Italy few tourists got to see. He could picture it now; the two of them sipping a glass of wine in an outdoor café, sharing a few kisses…

Damn. He couldn't even keep his hands off her in his daydreams. "I've already got enough friends. Besides, I'm not here to socialize. I'm here to get to know you better."

"No worries, Theo," Helena said. "Frankly, I'm in the mood for a little fun, too. And there's not much time left to make that happen."

THE MOON HUNG LOW in the sky; a big, round, yellow ball casting golden light on the water. After dropping off Sally at the Internet café, Trish had thought about calling Cassidy again, then remembered Angie and her family were celebrating Brent's birthday tonight. Trish consoled herself with the fact that at least she'd managed to speak with her daughter for a few minutes earlier in the day.

When the shops had failed to hold her interest, she'd wandered the ship, ending up on the top deck at the very front. It was a beautiful clear night and Trish lifted her face to the sky, searching out the brightest star. Though she knew it was silly, she closed her eyes and made a wish.

"I've been looking for you." A familiar voice sounded behind Trish.

Trish's eyes popped open and she whirled around. "I thought you were with your sister."

"She had plans," Theo said in a lighthearted tone. "Where's Sally?"

"At the Internet café," Trish said with a rueful smile. "E-mailing Bruno."

Theo moved to her side, standing so close she could feel the heat from his body. His eyes were dark, intense and very focused. "Those two really hit it off."

"You have no idea," Trish said with a heavy sigh.

Though she was excited for Sally, the other woman's happiness only underscored Trish's loneliness.

Theo's eyes looked almost black in the dim light. "Tell me."

"When you spoke to Bruno, did he happen to mention that he's planning to pick up Sally tomorrow?" Trish asked. "And not bring her back until the ship docks in Barcelona?"

"He did," Theo said, his expression giving nothing away.

"Sally said the children were going to be spending a week with his sister."

Theo nodded. "Anna and Isabella always stay with their Aunt Marianna for a week or two every summer."

Some of the tension in Trish's shoulders eased. While she still wasn't sure Sally was making a good decision, she was relieved Bruno appeared to be a responsible parent.

"I always vowed I'd never have a man even meet Cassidy unless I was sure he was going to be part of my life," Trish said.

Theo studied her for a long moment as if absorbing her words, then turned to the rail and stared out at the vast expanse of water.

"You look pretty tonight," he said after a moment, glancing over at her.

Though Trish had specifically chosen to wear her favorite dress tonight, hoping he'd notice, she found herself put off balance by the unexpected compliment. "You're looking pretty spiffy yourself."

The second the words left her lips she wished she could pull them back. Dear God, what was wrong with her? She felt as awkward and tongue-tied as a fifteen-year-old on her first date. Not only was she talking goofy—did anyone even use the word *spiffy* anymore?—she was blushing like a shy virgin.

"Well, now that we've determined we both look spiffy…"

Trish turned just in time to see the dimple in his left cheek flash.

"If you don't already have plans for tomorrow, there's a small town in Tuscany I'd like to show you," Theo said, his voice warm and smooth, like the finest chocolate. "I'm no expert but I've been there several times."

"I'd love to spend the day with you," Trish said. It didn't matter where they went—after all, she just needed access to Theo—but she was curious. "What's the name of this place?"

"Trying to decide if it's worth your time?" Theo teased.

"That's not it at all. I know we'll have a good time together."

Did she have to blurt it out like that?

"Thank you for the vote of confidence." She could

tell her words had pleased him. "Lucca is close to Florence. It's—"

"The birthplace of Puccini and probably best known for the earthen wall that surrounds it," Trish said as if reciting from a guidebook. "People say that going to Lucca and not cycling around its tree-lined walls is like going to Paris and not seeing the Eiffel Tower."

"I take it you're familiar with the city," Theo said.

"Actually I planned to go there a long time ago," Trish said, keeping her tone light. "Did a lot of research on it, but never made it there."

"I thought we'd rent some bikes. Take a ride on the wall. Interested?"

"Of course I'm interested." Excitement filling her voice. "Sally and I were just going to visit the Leaning Tower of Pisa but I've been there before."

"Sounds like we have agreement," he said.

Impulsively Trish stuck out her hand. "It's a deal."

Theo looked down at her hand but made no attempt to take it. When his eyes met hers once again, Trish knew she was in trouble.

"I've got a better idea how to seal this deal," he said. Without further warning, he lowered his lips to hers.

THE KISS STARTED OUT slowly as if they had all the time in the world. Theo's mouth brushed softly over hers with a teasing gentleness that ignited an inferno in her belly.

Parting her lips, Trish touched her tongue to his bottom lip. As she'd hoped, he immediately deepened the kiss. Heart hammering, she raised her hands, curling her fingers into the fabric of his shirt as she leaned into the kiss, her tongue fencing with his. Her heart picked up speed and an ache of longing filled her body.

With Theo's arms around her and his mouth covering hers, Trish reveled in the sensation of being completely surrounded by him. Her body tightened with a long forgotten tension, which became almost unbearable when his callused hands skimmed the sensitive skin of her back.

In a heartbeat, ache became want and everything faded except the need to feel more of him. Taste more of him. Touch more of him.

Her breath caught as his hand slid into her hair, sending hairpins flying to the deck floor and curls tumbling to her shoulders. A mixture of excitement and nervousness shivered through Trish as his fingers delved through the tangled mass at the nape of her neck and his thumbs grazed the soft skin beneath her jaw.

Time seemed suspended, and if he hadn't been holding her, Trish was certain she would have fallen.

But Theo's arms were strong and her burgeoning desire gave her courage. Trish dampened her lips with tongue. "Kiss me again."

She didn't need to ask twice. He took her mouth

in a lengthy, thorough kiss that made her head spin. Desire, hot and insistent and for so long forgotten, rushed through her. His hands slipped down to the small of her back, pulling her closer still. She could feel the heat of his body, the strong thud of his heart…and the rock hardness of his erection pressed against her.

A purr of pleasure rumbled in her throat and she wiggled her hips against him, sending waves of desire through her. He was an irresistible temptation and his hardened body inspired sensual images of him…and her…together.

Theo must have been viewing the same images because need glinted dark in his eyes. He gazed at her for a long moment then took her hand. "Let's go."

He didn't have to say where. Or why. The look in his eyes said it all. And it was just where her body wanted to go. But her head urged her to think before blindly following her desires. If they were alone, would she be able to resist the urge to strip off her clothes and make mad, passionate love to him? *Not a chance*.

Would she regret her impulsive actions? *Probably*. She heaved a heavy sigh.

"Problem?" he asked.

"I don't think that…" Trish paused, fighting the overpowering urge to throw caution to the wind and run—not walk—to his penthouse. She took a deep breath, steadying her nerves. "It's not a good idea for us to be alone. We both know what will happen."

Surprise blanketed Theo's face. "Isn't that what you want?"

Trish groaned. Why did he have to phrase it that way?

"It is, but it's not." She took a step back, putting needed distance between them. She knew she was acting and sounding like a flake, but his nearness made it difficult for her to think clearly. Perhaps she should just spit it out. "I think sleeping together is a bad idea."

For a split second he looked shocked, and Trish wondered with sudden horror if she'd completely misconstrued his intentions. Until she remembered the hard length of him pressed against her belly. No, he'd had more in mind than shaking hands or a few kisses on the couch.

"Why?"

Trish wasn't sure why the question caught her off guard. It was a completely logical response and that's what she was striving for—calm, rational logic.

"I'm very attracted to you," she said finally.

"And I'm attracted to you," he said.

The confusion in his eyes told her she still hadn't made herself clear. But that was no surprise considering the war going on inside her head. "I'm a businesswoman. A mother. I have responsibilities." With each declaration Trish felt her resolve strengthen. "I don't have the luxury of being impulsive and free-spirited anymore."

No need to tell him she'd never really been that way—even when she'd been younger.

Theo searched her face. "I don't want you in my bed if you don't want to be there, but I don't understand how being a businesswoman and mother precludes you from enjoying a man's—my—company."

But she wouldn't be just *enjoying* his company she'd be *having sex* with him. When she'd told herself she was going to have fun on this cruise, she'd envisioned a few moonlight kisses, not serious skin-to-skin action.

If she made love, she wanted it to mean something. And unlike Sally, she wasn't foolish enough to believe that she could have a serious relationship with someone who lived half-a-world away.

"I know it's confusing." Trish placed her hand on his arm, then immediately realized her mistake.

Testosterone rolled off him in waves. He smelled of soap and some indefinable, warm male scent that made something tighten low in her belly.

For a second, she was tempted to reconsider. After all, she'd resolved to have fun this trip. Maybe she *could* handle a sex-only relationship…

She was still wavering when Theo leaned forward,

brushed a chaste kiss against her forehead and spun her toward the stairs.

"You'd better go," he said. "Before I forget I'm supposed to be a gentleman and decide to do whatever is necessary to change your mind."

"It really would have been a bad idea," Trish repeated, wondering which one of them she was trying to convince. As she walked slowly down the stairs, she remembered the desire simmering in his gaze and an ache of longing for what might have been rose up inside her.

All the way to her room, she couldn't help but wonder what tricks he'd had up his sleeve and how much resistance she'd have put up before she said yes.

CHAPTER THIRTEEN

THERE WAS NO SOUND coming from the cabin so Trish gently eased the door open, hoping Sally was asleep. She was still shaky over what had almost happened on deck and the last thing she wanted to do was talk about it with her friend.

When Trish stepped inside the room she realized her luck hadn't changed. Sally's half-packed suitcases lay open on the floor and every light in the room blazed.

So much for slipping into bed unnoticed.

The sound of running water filtered through the closed bathroom door and Trish gave it two brisk raps as she walked by. "I'm back."

When she'd been in Theo's arms, she'd felt completely, utterly alive with enough stamina to go until dawn. But all that energy seemed to have deserted her and Trish plopped down on her bed, suddenly drained. She didn't even lift her head when she heard the door to the bathroom open.

"I didn't think you'd come home tonight," Sally said.

"Where else would I be?" Certainly not with Theo, Trish thought with a pang of regret. No, she was much too sensible for that. Exhaling a heavy sigh, she glanced up at Sally.

She jerked upright. "Eek! What have you done with my friend, strange creature?"

Except for her eyes and mouth, Sally's face was completely covered with thick green mud.

"Don't make me laugh," Sally said, her mouth barely moving. "This mask can't be disturbed for at least ten more minutes."

"If only Bruno was here," Trish teased. Besides having a green face, her friend had pulled her hair to the top of her head in a scrunchie and blond tufts sprouted out in every direction. "Seeing you in Incredible Hulk mode might make him change his mind about spending time with you."

"I told you not to make me laugh," Sally said, trying not to giggle. "And he's not going to see me like this because I'm leaving the mud behind for you."

There was a finality in Sally's tone that Trish picked up on immediately.

"You're really doing it." Trish kept her tone light, reminding herself she was Sally's friend, not her mother.

"Of course." Sally sounded surprised. "Don't tell me you honestly thought I'd change my mind?"

Hoped, not thought. Trish wanted to say. But she bit the words back and tried a different tactic. "Aren't you the least bit worried about getting your heart broken by that handsome Italian?"

Sally crossed the room and dropped down on her bed, pulling her legs up under her. "I know it's a possibility, but I'm willing to take the risk."

"But—"

"No buts," Sally said firmly, her chin setting in a stubborn tilt. "I'm thirty-seven years old and I've never been in love. How pathetic is that? I like Bruno and I enjoy his company. If this ends with my heart being broken, so be it. I won't have any regrets."

"I'm happy for you, Sal, I really am." Trish still thought Sally was headed for heartache, but the conviction in her friend's tone told Trish that no matter what happened, Sally would land on her feet.

"What about you?" Sally asked, focusing on Trish's hair, which lay in a disheveled mess around her shoulders. "Rod told me his friend saw you and Theo getting all cozy up on the top deck."

Trish fought back a blush, thankful they'd stopped at kissing. Public displays of affection had never been her thing, but when Theo had pulled her into his arms, she'd forgotten everything except him.

"Well?" Sally asked. "What's the scoop?"

"I thought you'd blown the dentist off." Trish bought herself a few more seconds to decide how much she was going to tell.

"I ran into him as I was leaving the computer lab,"

Sally said. "But I don't want to talk about him. I want to hear about you and Theo."

Trish picked at the lightweight blanket covering her bed, then forced a smile. "He asked me up to his penthouse." She deliberately kept her tone light. "I told him no. After all, this is your last night on the ship…"

"Patricia Melrose." Sally straightened and her eyes flashed. "I don't need a babysitter and you know it. You march right up to that penthouse and tell him you lost your mind for a moment but now you've found it."

"Calm down," Trish said. "That wasn't why I said no."

"What other excuse—reason—could there be?"

Sally's tone might be light, but her gaze was sharp and assessing. Trish chose her words carefully. "You know I promised myself when Steven and I divorced that I wasn't going to be one of those mothers whose boyfriends came before their child. Cassidy is my priority."

"But you date," Sally said. "Remember that guy last summer? Nick something-or-other?"

"Nick was a nice enough guy, but he wanted more time than I had to give," Trish admitted, remembering the personable programmer. "Lunch and the occasional movie was fine. But he wanted to be with me all the time. It interfered with my time with Cassidy."

Her mother had told Trish if she'd liked Nick

more, she'd have found a way to make the relationship work without shortchanging Cassidy.

"That's why this situation with Theo has such potential," Sally said, her voice turning persuasive.
"You have the time now and anything that goes on
between the two of you would be so…anonymous.
Remember the saying 'what happens in the Mediterranean stays in the Mediterranean'?"

"I think you mean Vegas."

"Whatever." Sally waved a dismissive hand.
"Theo turns you on, right?"

Though Trish told herself she shouldn't even consider what Sally was proposing, she found herself mull-
ing over the idea. She'd been in her sexual prime when
she'd married Steven, but their love life had left a lot
to be desired. At the time she'd thought it was her in-
experience. But time and distance had given her the ob-
jectivity to realize she'd been shortchanged by a man
who hadn't cared enough to make sex good for her.

What was even sadder was that once she returned to Miami, she'd be in mother-mode for the
next ten years or so with no time to make up for
what she'd missed.

There's time now.

"Trish," Sally said a bit more insistently. "Admit
it, the guy turns you on."

Trish reluctantly nodded, hoping she wouldn't
regret the admission.

At Sally's look of satisfaction, Trish had the feeling she'd fallen neatly into a trap. Her friend tilted her head. "And he's not expecting anything permanent?"

"That would be impossible," Trish insisted.

"So, there's really nothing to decide," Sally said.

While Sally had addressed her main concerns, Trish still hesitated. "I don't know, Sal—"

"Go to him. If you don't, you'll regret it." Sally leaned forward and took Trish's hands. "Trust me. Regret is worse than a broken heart any day."

THEO TOOK A SIP of wine and gazed out over the Mediterranean. With the full moon and a million stars overhead, the balcony of his penthouse was definitely *the* place to be on this beautiful summer night.

It was just too bad he was alone. If only Trish were at his side, the evening would be perfect. When Theo had returned to his suite, he'd forced her from his thoughts then tried to relax.

Thankfully, from the living room with its soft leather furniture and plasma TV, to the whirlpool for six in the bathroom, the penthouse had been designed with comfort in mind. He stretched. A man could get used to such luxury.

A knock sounded at the door just as he finished his glass of wine. Though he was perfectly capable of attending to his own personal needs, the butler insisted on coming every night to turn down the bed.

"Come in," Theo called out, reaching over and re-filling his glass from the bottle next to his chair. "Door's open."

He took another sip of wine. After a moment he heard the door click open and soft footsteps cross the room. Theo didn't even turn his head. He knew from experience that the man would soon be gone. Then he would be once again alone…except for thoughts of Trish. Theo leaned back in his chair and closed his eyes. For a second he swore he could smell the light scent of her perfume.

Theo's lips curved up in a smile. The taste of those soft, sweet lips had only whetted his appetite for more. And by the desire in her eyes, he hadn't been the only one affected. He'd been shocked when she'd turned him away. Still, if he was being honest, he'd have to admit that mixed with his shock was relief.

While he knew becoming involved with her wasn't wise, he'd been willing to take the risk. When she stood close to him, it was as if nothing else mattered but her.

"Theo?"

His eyes flew open and he jerked upright. The remaining wine in his glass headed seaward. "Trish?"

He jumped to his feet and turned. She stood in the doorway to the balcony, wearing the same green dress she'd had on earlier, her hair still hanging loose. Only the determined glint in her eyes was new.

"I thought you were the butler," he said stupidly.

She glanced down at the cleavage revealed by the V-neck of her dress. "It's been a few years since anyone mistook me for a guy."

Theo smiled and placed his now-empty wineglass onto a side table.

She followed his movement, those intense hazel eyes lingering on his bare chest. When her gaze traveled lower to his black silk boxers, Theo's body started to hum. It appeared the boring night alone that he'd anticipated had taken a sudden turn for the better. Or was that only wishful thinking? "What are you doing here?"

The minute the words left his mouth, Theo cursed his gaucheness.

"I still think us sleeping together is a bad idea."

He fought to hide his disappointment. "You came all the way up here to tell me that?"

"No." Trish smiled for the first time since she'd walked into the room. Without missing a beat, she dropped her bag on an overstuffed chair and kicked off her shoes. "I came to tell you I don't care if it is a bad idea."

For a second, Theo thought he was hallucinating. But when her hand moved to her zipper and her dress fell to the floor, Theo knew this was no dream. This was fantasy come to life.

DISROBING IN FRONT of Theo had been a bold move, but Trish wanted to make it clear she wasn't playing games. She'd decided what she wanted, and when she'd seen Theo standing there clad only in those boxers, she knew she'd made the right decision.

Dear God, he was magnificent. Broad shoulders, taut abs, narrow waist and long muscular legs. A dusting of dark hair covered his chest then tapered down to the waistband of his boxers.

"You are so beautiful." Theo moved close, his gaze focused on the cleavage spilling over the lace of her demicup.

Trish stepped forward and wound her arms around his neck, surprising herself. During the years she was with Steven, she'd learned to let him initiate any love-making. But Trish had the feeling Theo wouldn't be threatened by a woman going after what she wanted.

"We should take this slow. Savor each step." Theo had barely finished speaking when his lips closed over hers, the gentle kiss stoking the fire burning inside her.

He pulled her close and her nipples rubbed against his bare chest, adding an ache to the fire. His strong fingers caressed her back before moving upward, sliding under her hair, then brushing the thick curls aside. The feel of his mouth against the nape of her neck made her shiver.

"Are you sure this is what you want?" he asked softly, his fingers moving down to toy with the clasp of her bra.

Her body ached for his touch and she had no doubt he'd be a wonderful lover. But was this really what she wanted? Even before she'd married she hadn't been into brief, meaningless affairs. Just because no one would know didn't make it right.

She talked to her daughter all the time about making good choices. Was she making a good choice tonight?

"Theo." Trish swallowed hard, her body thrumming with nerves. "I—"

The knock at the door might as well have been a gunshot. Trish jerked back, her gaze darting downward to where her dress lay pooled at her feet. But before she could grab her clothes and flee, Theo grabbed her arm and shook his head, bringing a finger to his lips.

"Who is it?" he called out.

"Mario, sir. I've come to turn down your bed."

"Not tonight, Mario."

"But, sir—"

"Not tonight," Theo repeated, his tone brooking no argument.

"Very well, Mr. Catomeris," the butler said through the closed door. "Have a good night, sir."

"Thanks, Mario."

Theo's arms encircled Trish once again and he planted kisses interspersed with little nips up the side of her neck. "I am definitely planning on having a good night."

But as much as Trish wanted to give in to the sensations sweeping her body, she placed her hands against his chest and pushed him back. "I can't, Theo."

His brows pulled together in puzzlement. "Can't what?"

"I don't know what I was thinking." Trish leaned over and picked up her dress. "I can't make love with you. You're a client."

It wasn't the whole story but she doubted he was interested in debating the morality of one-night stands at this late hour.

"You forget." He brushed back a lock of hair from her face and tucked it behind an ear, his eyes dark with desire. "I'm not working for Liberty anymore so technically I'm not your client."

"But you might change—"

"Don't worry about that," he said without any hesitation, "I won't be changing my mind."

The certainty behind those words threatened the hope that Trish had held tight these past days. Images of Twyla and her son, James and his family brought a lump to her throat, followed swiftly by hot anger at the unfairness of it all. "You don't care, do you?"

By the look in his eyes, he was now totally confused. "Don't care about what?"

About anyone but yourself. Trish swallowed the angry words that lay poised on the tip of her tongue and took several deep breaths. That wasn't really fair to Theo. Besides, if she said any more she might ruin any chance she had of changing his mind.

"I'm sorry I charged in here and screwed up your evening," Trish said instead.

"You didn't screw up anything," Theo assured her. "Though I don't understand why you changed your mind. If you're worried about Mario coming back, don't be. He—"

"It's not Mario," Trish said, pulling on her dress. "It's me. I…this…was a mistake."

Theo stared at her for a long moment but didn't argue or try to change her mind. "What about tomorrow?"

Trish couldn't hide her surprise. "You still want me to come?"

"I'll stop by your cabin and pick you up." A gleam of mischief filled Theo's eyes. "Unless you'd like to sleep over? It'll save you a few minutes in the morning."

"I don't think so." Trish tightened the belt of the dress then slid her feet in her heels. "It's a matter of trust."

"You don't trust me?" Theo asked, the affronted look on his face tempered by the teasing glint in his eyes.

"No," Trish said. "I don't trust myself."

With those words, she turned on her heel and headed for the door.

CHAPTER FOURTEEN

LAST NIGHT when Trish had left the penthouse she'd worried Theo might hold her flaky behavior against her. Until he'd showed up this morning with a bouquet of flowers in hand.

Of course she'd had her own surprise. When they'd gotten to the dock, a car had been waiting.

"A few quick calls," Trish teased with a dismissive wave.

"What a woman," Theo said. "Smart and beautiful."

Trish just smiled. "Keep talking and you'll get anything you want."

"I already have what I want." Unexpectedly Theo leaned over and slanted a kiss across her mouth. "A sunny day. A beautiful woman. And a Peugeot."

Warmth flowed through Trish and she realized everything between them was back to normal. She resisted the urge to touch her tingling lips as Theo wheeled the car from the lot.

"It shouldn't take long to get to Lucca," Trish said. "What is it, only about fifty kilometers from Livorno?"

"About that."

"Since it's so close, it would make a nice day excursion." Trish pulled a notebook from her bag and made a few notes. "The driver could stop in Pisa either on the way there or back so the tourists could see the Leaning Tower."

"Always working." Theo grinned. "Don't you ever relax?"

"I relax," Trish said, trying not to sound indignant. "It's just that this is a business trip and I want to take advantage of every opportunity."

"I bet even when you're at home, you're always working."

"Wrong. Once I'm home, I try to forget about work and concentrate on Cassidy."

Theo shot a glance sideways. "Tell me about her."

Trish hesitated. Though she didn't want to bore him with tales of her daughter's brilliance, she swore there was a spark of genuine interest in his eyes. "She's eight. In September she'll start third grade."

"Just a year older than Bruno's Isabella," Theo said. "In the picture I saw, she had dark hair, not red."

She wondered what he was really asking. Does she look like you? Or her father?

"Her hair might be dark, but it has a definite red cast," Trish said. "Actually most people say Cassidy is a mini-me, except for Steven's blue eyes."

Since the divorce, Trish had been determined to

have an amicable relationship with Steven and usually didn't have trouble talking about him. But today it felt weird.

"You mentioned that you share custody," Theo said. "Is he very involved in her life?"

"He is." Whatever his other failings, her ex was a good father. "Steven has her about fifty percent of the time. In fact he would have taken Cassidy this week if he hadn't been out of town for a business convention."

"Do you like him being around so much?" Theo's tone seemed a little too casual to Trish's discerning ears.

She wasn't sure if he was trying to determine if she hated her ex or was still hung up on him. Either way, honesty was the best response.

"It can be hard at times," Trish admitted. "But Cassidy adores him and I try to keep her best interests in mind."

The look in Theo's eyes reminded Trish of a brewing thunderstorm. But when he spoke, his tone was nonchalant. "How can you see him and act as if nothing had happened? He *cheated* on you."

For a second Trish toyed with the idea of changing the subject. But Theo's quiet restraint as he waited for her response told Trish the answer was important to him.

"He never really loved me." Only recently had

Trish been able to voice that truth without feeling an overwhelming sense of sadness and regret.

Theo reached over and took her hand, his thumb gently caressing the soft flesh. When he met her gaze, it was his eyes that held anger, not hers.

"You were his wife," Theo said. "He cheated on you. He is the one who should feel bad, not you."

"Steven's first wife died of cancer a couple years before we met." Trish still remembered the day she'd realized Steven didn't love her, had never loved her. "I should have seen that he was still grieving. But I was young and stupid. Looking back I wonder if I was more in love with the idea of being in love than I was with…"

The man had asked a simple question. He didn't need a dissertation on the ups and downs of her failed marriage.

"I hate it that he hurt you," Theo said.

The caring underlying his words sent warmth flowing through Trish's veins.

"Even after I realized that Steven had never got over Karen, I thought we could make it work." Trish had wanted so much for them to be close. "Steven was a good man. Even if he didn't love me, I knew he cared about me. And by then we had Cassidy. I was determined to win his love and save my marriage."

She'd been so idealistic back then…so unrealistic. Trish glanced at Theo to make sure he was listening, then continued. "The crazy thing was the more I tried to build that closeness, the more he backed off. Then, I discovered he'd turned to another woman. A woman who didn't place unreasonable demands on his emotions, according to him."

The infidelity had been the nail in the coffin. His harsh words when she'd confronted him had destroyed any last remnants of romantic feelings.

Theo squeezed her hand. "I'm sorry. That had to have hurt."

Trish studied the man beside her. There was depth, understanding and intelligence in his dark-as-midnight eyes.

"It did." But looking back, she realized that mixed with the shock and disbelief had been a healthy dose of relief. Steven had chosen his course of action. She no longer had to try to make their marriage work. "After the divorce was final, he came and asked for my forgiveness. It was hard but I realized that I had to let go of my anger."

"I don't understand."

"Anger and bitterness would only poison my life as well as Cassidy's," Trish said simply.

It was the first time she'd told anyone the full story of what had happened and it felt good.

"You're a special woman, Trish Melrose." There was admiration in his voice.

"I'm a survivor," Trish said, then her eyes widened. "Hey, isn't that the turnoff for Pisa?"

"Want to stop and have breakfast?" Theo asked. "We have time."

"Sure." Trish searched her memory. "There should be a place that we've used as a tour stop not far from the Piazza dei Miracoli. I'd love to check it out."

"Piazza dei Miracoli, it is," Theo said, turning the car toward Pisa.

Once they reached the piazza, Theo parked the car. He rested his hand on the small of her back as they walked to the restaurant entrance.

"You know my mother never did let go of her anger toward Elias Stamos," Theo murmured as he opened the door. "She wanted me to hate him as much as she did."

"And do you?" Trish asked. "Hate him, I mean?"

"I did," Theo said matter-of-factly. "I blamed him for my mother leaving me. I thought if he'd only given her some money we could have been together. She wouldn't have had to take that job in Athens."

Trish had many questions, but by then the proprietor had hurried over to show them to a table. The female server appeared almost immediately. Although Trish didn't speak Italian, by the look in the woman's eyes and her demeanor, she knew the waitress hadn't hurried over for her.

But Theo gave no indication he'd noticed the

woman's interest, and the moment she'd finished taking their order, he immediately switched his attention back to Trish.

"Did you know that the Tower of Pisa's construction began back in 1173 and continued for about two hundred years?" Trish had visited the tower before Cassidy was born but hadn't been back since. The basics were about all she remembered.

"That's true," Theo said with an approving smile. "Construction was completed in 1350 but the builders knew as early as 1178 that the tower was leaning. It wasn't until 1275 that architect Tommso di Andrea da Pontedera realized that the leaning tower couldn't be straightened."

"How do you know all that?" Trish asked, amazed.

"I've always been interested in architecture," Theo said with a slight smile. "I also read a lot when I was a child."

Trish had a sudden image of him at home alone while his grandparents worked at the restaurant. "I can't understand it," she said with unexpected fervor. "The man has billions. Even if he didn't like your mother, how could he not have supported his own son?"

"Like I said, I used to hate him." Theo smiled his thanks as the waitress set two cups of cappuccino in front of them.

"What changed?" Trish took a sip of the espresso infused with steamed milk.

"For one thing, I discovered from Katherine and Helena that my father did pay support when I was growing up."

Trish set her cup down. "How could that be? You just said he didn't."

"Obviously my mother kept it all for herself," Theo said, his voice heavy with disappointment.

"How could she?" Trish said. "There has to be some other explanation."

"Tasia never wanted to be a mother," he said. "I was a mistake, something that should never have happened. Apparently she just made the best of a bad situation."

Though his tone was nonchalant, a hint of sadness flickered in his eyes and Trish's heart twisted. She reached across the table and impulsively covered his hand with hers. "Well, I for one am glad you're here."

He made no move to pull his hand away, and in the warmth of the moment Trish realized she couldn't remember the last time she'd felt so close to a man.

"One thing I can't understand. Even if she didn't want me," Theo said almost to himself, "how could she have put such a burden on her own parents."

Because she's obviously selfish and only out for herself, Trish wanted to say. But she took the high road instead.

"It's hard to know what drives people. The important thing is you're now able to view the situation from the perspective of a man, not a child."

He lifted a dark brow. "Meaning?"

"Just because she hates your father doesn't mean you have to hate him, too." Trish challenged him to look away. "Have you ever thought about talking to him? Listening to his side? Maybe if you got to know him, you could understand, maybe even forgive. Perhaps it's time to give Elias Stamos a second chance."

CHAPTER FIFTEEN

A SECOND CHANCE.

The words ran through Theo's head. While he may have been toying with the idea of contacting his father since his conversation with Katherine and Helena, Trish's suggestion sent red flags popping up.

Theo pulled his hand away and started to respond just as the waitress arrived with their food.

"Is it my welfare that interests you?" Theo asked bluntly when the woman was out of earshot. "Or are you hoping that if Stamos and I work out our differences, I might sign your contract?"

Trish looked down for several heartbeats. When she raised her eyes to look at him, Theo was surprised to see tears in them.

"Your mother deliberately turned you against your father. I can't imagine what it would be like if Steven poisoned Cassidy against me." Her voice caught. "That would break my heart."

"You have to remember," he said, pushing at the

frittata with his fork. "Elias Stamos is no victim here. He could have contacted me."

"Would you have listened?" Trish asked.

Theo started to answer then stopped himself. Trish had been honest with him and deserved the same in return. He thought for a moment then shook his head. "I don't think so."

"I don't have all the answers. And I don't know everything that has gone on in your family." Trish's eyes were dark with compassion. "But just consider being the bigger man here. That's all I'm saying."

Consider it? Little did she know that the thought had been niggling at him since his sisters had first contacted him weeks ago. But every time the idea had surfaced, Theo had determinedly shoved it aside. Maybe he did need to confront Elias Stamos. But the time wasn't right. Not yet anyway.

"How about we head to Lucca?" Theo pushed his untouched plate of food aside, no longer hungry. "I'm in the mood for some fresh air."

THEO HAD BEEN TENSE and quiet when they'd returned to the car. Though he'd gone along with her request to visit the Leaning Tower before leaving Pisa, their earlier camaraderie seemed to have vanished. Trish began to wonder if the rest of the day was doomed. But once they started on the road to Northern Tuscany, the tension eased from his face.

By the time they reached Lucca, rented their bikes and started pedaling, things felt almost back to normal.

"Did you know that this wall is almost twenty meters thick?" Trish cast a sideways glance at Theo, keeping her hands firmly positioned on the bike's handlebars. "And that Julius Caesar is said to have walked this same route in 85 B.C.?"

"You sound like a tour guide," Theo said with a smile.

"I am a tour guide," she said with a laugh. "Or rather that's how I started out in the business."

"Do you miss it?" Theo asked.

Trish thought for a moment. "Sometimes. I liked being out and meeting new people, taking them to places they'd never seen. Or showing them a place they'd been to many times but getting them to see it in a new way."

"Have you ever thought of doing it again?"

"No," Trish said. "At least not until Cassidy is grown. I'd be gone too much and that's not a sacrifice I'm willing to make."

They rode silently for a minute before Theo spoke again. "Cassidy is lucky to have a mother like you."

"Thank you, Theo." A warmth filled Trish's heart at the compliment. "That's such a nice thing to say."

"I mean it." Theo focused on the road ahead. "Most women would choose their career over their children any day."

"I don't believe that." Trish edged her bike closer to his to make room for two chattering women walking in the opposite direction. "I think most women want to spend time with their kids. If they're gone, it's because they have to be."

"We'll have to agree to disagree on this one," Theo said. "Let's stop here."

He gestured with his head toward a clearing in a grove of trees just off the path. Trish wheeled her bike in behind him and braked to a stop. She brushed her hair back from her face with the back of her hand, her body humming with excitement.

Years ago Trish had dreamed of taking this ride. Of picnicking on top of the ancient wall. Of drinking wine and eating bread and cheese under the shade of the trees. And now that day had finally arrived…thanks to Theo.

When she and Theo had first arrived in the small picturesque town, he'd insisted they stop at a local store. Once inside he'd purchased a bottle of wine, along with some bread and cheese and a lightweight blanket. Trish had brought along a couple of backpacks, so he'd put the food and wine in his while she'd packed the blanket in hers.

Even dressed like a tourist in green cargo shorts and a tan T-shirt, Theo gave new meaning to the words tall, dark and handsome. And his eyes…well, when he glanced her way her knees grew weak and her skin warmed despite the tree's shade.

"If you want to spread the blanket, I'll open the wine." Theo removed two carefully wrapped wine-glasses from his backpack with oh-so-gentle hands.

Trish's mouth went dry imagining the feel of those strong, yet gentle hands against her skin. Business luncheon, she reminded herself. This was strictly business.

With that thought firmly in mind she removed the blanket and spread it on the grass. By the time she'd smoothed the last wrinkle out she felt composed and firmly in control of her emotions. Putting her hands on her hips, she surveyed her surroundings. "This would be a great excursion for seniors as well as more active younger adults."

She didn't have to close her eyes to picture older passengers strolling down the path and the younger ones jogging or biking…all enjoying the view of the huge meadow surrounding the wall.

The look he shot her threatened to short-circuit her good sense.

"Sit." Theo pulled the cheese and crusted bread from his backpack. "And not one word about work. You, Mrs. Melrose, need to learn to relax."

Trish chuckled and took a seat next to him on the blanket. "And I suppose you're the one to teach me?"

"I just may be." Theo poured a splash of wine

into a glass and handed it to Trish. As she took it from him, her fingers brushed against his.

Electricity sizzled. Trish looked up, and before she knew what was happening, she found herself drowning in the liquid depths of his eyes. An older man walking down the path called out a greeting as he passed but she barely noticed.

The beautiful landscape faded into the background. The only thing Trish knew was Theo: his look, his touch, his laugh.

By the time she finished the second glass of wine, the afternoon had slipped away. She couldn't remember the last time she'd enjoyed a day so much, and she knew it was all because of Theo.

"What's that expression?" Theo asked. "Penny for your thoughts?"

For a moment Trish could only stare. She wondered what he'd say if she blurted out the truth—that she could easily see herself falling in love with him. His eyes would turn wary and that easy smile would freeze on his lips. Because he was a nice guy, he'd say something about caring for her, too. Then he'd change the subject.

"Trish?"

With a start, Trish realized Theo was waiting for an answer. Her mind searched for a one-liner that would make him laugh. Unfortunately none came immediately to mind.

"I was just thinking what a good time I'm having."

He smiled and his shoulders relaxed. For one crazy second Trish had the feeling he'd been worried about her response.

"I've had a great time, too," he said. "In fact, I hate to see the day end."

"I wish we could stay and stroll with the locals in the *passeggiata*," Trish said, her tone turning wistful. In the evening the wall served as a promenade for the village people and the tourists to leisurely walk together. "Steven and I talked about coming here for our fifth anniversary. But he'd already moved on by then."

Theo caught the glimpse of pain in the hazel depths of Trish's eyes. Hot anger rose inside him. How any man could hurt such a wonderful woman was beyond his comprehension.

He longed to tell her that she would never be sorry she'd met *him*, but he knew words were pointless. Instead, he leaned over and took her hand. "I wish I could stroll with you in the *passeggiata*."

Her lips reminded him of sweet, ripe strawberries, and though he'd told himself to keep his hands to himself, a sudden urge to see if her lips tasted as sweet as they looked tugged at his resolve.

As if she could read his mind, Trish moistened her lips with the tip of her tongue. Theo groaned and she looked worried.

"Are you okay?"

Almost of its own volition, his hand rose to cup her face.

"I will be soon." Theo leaned over and covered her mouth with his. Her lips tasted as sweet as he'd imagined but he discovered one taste was not going to be enough. Not for him. And not for Trish, either, judging by her response. She kissed him back, her mouth molding eagerly against his as her arms wrapped around his neck. They kissed for the longest time, kissed until the feelings stirring inside Theo warned him that they'd better stop.

Trish sighed as his mouth left hers, a soft regretful sound that nudged at Theo's already tenuous control. Still, he forced himself to sit back and tried to ignore his racing heart. "I think it's time we head back to Livorno."

"I don't want to go back yet," Trish sighed.

Neither did Theo. Surrounded by the heady scent of her sweet perfume, he wanted nothing more than to lay her back on the blanket and make slow, sweet love to her. It was that very desire that propelled him to his feet.

Trish was a business associate, a woman who'd been hurt by a man who'd taken what she'd offered and then walked away. He would not hurt her. He. Would. Not.

"We have to leave." He knew he sounded regretful. "Or we'll miss the ship."

Trish took his hand and fought a surge of disappointment. The day had been filled with magic and she hated to see it end.

It wasn't just kissing Theo that had contributed to the magic. She'd enjoyed the conversation they'd shared too. She'd never realized how much they had in common.

They both loved children and believed caring for them should be a priority. Knowing Theo's background, she shouldn't have found that surprising, but his admission that he still hoped to have a family of his own someday had tugged at her heartstrings.

She'd visualized them raising their children together, making a house a home. He would help her with Paws and Hands Together and she would help him with the Wild Horse Project. But the evenings would be *their* time. And late at night, nestled in her husband's arms, she'd thank God for sending her the man of her dreams.

She blinked away the image and realized that she was only kidding herself. When the cruise ended, she'd go back to Florida. Theo would stay in Corfu. There would be no comforting arms at the end of a hard day. No hugs or kisses.

But he was here now…

"How about one more kiss?" Trish asked in a husky voice.

"How can I say no to that offer?" Theo stepped forward and wrapped his arms around her. And when his lips closed over hers, Trish let herself imagine for just one more moment that this day, this closeness, could last forever.

CHAPTER SIXTEEN

THOUGH TRISH WOULD HAVE LIKED to get to know Helena Stamos better, when Theo invited her to have dinner with him and his sister after their trip to Lucca, she declined the offer. She'd had Theo to herself all day. He was on the ship to get to know Helena, and the two needed time alone.

Trish could have eaten in the dining room with the dentist and the newlyweds but the day's events had left her exhausted and more than a little confused.

When Theo had accused her of encouraging a reconciliation with his father for her own gain, she'd been stunned. But she had to admit that having Theo and Stamos come to some sort of understanding would be of benefit to her business. Because then Theo would have no reason *not* to work for Liberty Line.

Still, a part of her sensed that Theo wasn't ready for such a reconciliation. And she, more than most, realized what happened when you tried to rush people…

Trish placed her glass of tea on the table, and

gazed out over the Mediterranean, pushing the troublesome thought aside. Ordering room service and having dinner on her deck had been the perfect cap to a wonderful day.

She glanced down at her watch. Only eight-thirty, which made it just three-thirty Florida time. Normally Trish would wait until later to call Cassidy. But she and her daughter had always been on the same wavelength, and right now Trish had a strong feeling her daughter needed to speak to her.

Trish slipped her hand into her pocket and pulled out her cell phone. Before she could punch in a single number, it began to vibrate then ring. She smiled, recognizing the distinctive tone.

"Angie," Trish said. "I was just about to—"

"Trish." The word came out on a sob. "It's Cassidy. She's, she's—"

"Angie, give me the phone." Trish heard her brother-in-law's voice in the background.

"No. She's my sister. I need to tell her—" Angie's voice broke.

Trish's heart froze. Her fingers clenched the phone in a death grip. "What's wrong? Is Cassidy okay?"

"She's gone," Angie wailed. "We can't find her."

The world closed in around Trish, suffocating her.

"Can't find her?" Trish's voice grew louder with each word. "What do you mean?"

"She was right behind me," Angie said, her voice

trembling with emotion. "I stopped to buy everyone lemonade, and when I turned she was gone."

Trish's heart came back to life with a vengeance, slamming against her rib cage with such force that she felt light-headed. "How long has she been missing?"

"No more than ten minutes," Angie said. "We've already talked to security and they activated the Disney version of an Amber Alert."

Trish had been trying to tell herself that Cassidy had just wandered off. But if the staff felt the need to call an Amber Alert…

"They think someone took her?" Trish's voice rose then broke. Tears slid down her cheeks.

"We don't know." Angie cleared her throat but her voice remained shaky. "When we told the worker that we'd already looked for Cassidy, they said it was best to react quickly…just in case."

At the thought of some…some sicko touching sweet, innocent Cassidy… For a second the room spun but Trish willed herself not to faint. She needed to stay strong for Cassidy. "I'm coming home."

"Trish, this is Tom." Her brother-in-law's voice, strong and sure, filled the phone. "I'm asking you to stay put. I didn't want Angie to call you until we found Cassidy, but she insisted. Cassidy's probably somewhere close and doesn't even know we're looking for her."

"What if she's not?" Trish demanded. "What if she's hurt and scared and I'm...I'm not there?"

"Give me an hour," Tom said. "I'll call you when we find her and let you know she's safe."

"*If* you find her." Guilt flooded every fiber of Trish's being. "This never would have happened if I'd stayed home."

"It's our fault, not yours," Tom said, his voice heavy.

Though Trish wished she had someone else to blame, in her heart she knew Angie and Tom were good parents, and they would watch over Cassidy as if she were their own. "It's not your fault," Trish said. "But please, please call me as soon as you hear *anything*."

"I promise." Tom paused. "What about Steven? Are you going to call him?"

Trish pushed herself to her feet, too restless to sit any longer. "He's hard to reach. By the time I'd get through, she'll be back."

Hopefully.

"Trish." Angie's voice sounded on the other end of the phone. "Sally is there with you, isn't she? I don't want you to wait alone."

Trish took a deep breath. She didn't want to lie to her sister but Angie had enough to worry about. "I'm not alone."

"Good," Angie said, and Trish could hear the relief in her sister's voice. "We'll find her. We...we have to find her."

Somehow Trish managed to say goodbye and close the phone before she dropped into a nearby chair.

Then, folding her hands, she closed her eyes and began to pray.

THEO KNOCKED AGAIN, this time a little harder, on Trish's cabin door. He'd looked for her in the dining room earlier but her chair had been empty.

Helena had noticed he was distracted and had sent him on his way immediately after dinner. Instead of returning to the penthouse, he headed straight for Trish's cabin. He couldn't believe she wasn't inside. Unless she'd gone to an early show in the theatre…

Disappointed, he turned to go when he heard a sound coming from inside the cabin. He stopped and listened for a moment, then moved closer and placed his ear against the door. Only then did he recognize the sound. It was a woman crying. It was *Trish* crying.

"Trish." He pounded a fist against the door, ignoring a curious look from a couple walking down the hall. "It's Theo. Open the door. Let me in."

For several long seconds, nothing happened. He was ready to break the door down, when it suddenly swung open.

Trish's eyes were red-rimmed and her face blotchy. But it was the despair in her eyes that affected him most.

"Trish, *koukla*, why are you crying?" Without

waiting for an invitation, Theo stepped inside, letting the door shut behind him. "What's wrong?"

He opened his arms to her and she took a couple steps forward. When he held her close, she began to sob.

"Tell me what's got you so upset." Gentling his tone even more, Theo stroked her hair. "I can't make it better if you don't tell me the problem."

"It's Cassidy," Trish said between sobs. "She's gone."

"What do you mean *gone*?" Theo asked, trying to keep his tone even.

"She was with my sister and her family at Disney World," Trish said in a shaky voice. "They turned around and she was gone."

Theo had never met the little girl, but after seeing her picture and listening to Trish's stories, he felt as if he already knew her. He took a steadying breath. "Did they call the police?"

"They notified Security right away," Trish said. "Tom—he's my brother-in-law—he says they'll find her."

Theo could tell Trish was clinging to that hope so he agreed heartily. "I'm sure that's true."

"I told him if they haven't found her in an hour, I'm flying back." Trish lifted her face to his, a determined glint in her eyes. "I don't care what it takes to make that happen."

"If it comes to that—which I'm sure it won't—"

Theo brushed a strand of hair back from her face "—I'll do whatever I can to help you."

"Thank you, Theo. I just feel so alone, so helpless."

"You're not alone." Theo put his hands on her shoulders and looked her straight in the eye. "I'm right here and I'm not going anywhere."

"I can't tell you how much that means to me," Trish said. "I—"

The ring of her phone stopped her words, and a mixture of hope and panic skittered across Trish's face.

"Aren't you going to answer it?"

He slid an arm around her shoulders and she flipped her phone open.

"Hello." Theo could feel Trish's body go slack beneath his arm. "Cassidy," she breathed. "Mommy was *so* scared."

At that moment, Theo knew everything was going to be okay.

SHORTLY AFTER SNUGGLING next to him on the sofa, Trish fell into an exhausted slumber, a smile still on her lips. Theo let her sleep, knowing she'd survived a horrible fright and needed to recharge.

Trish had talked to Cassidy, then her sister and brother-in-law, then Cassidy again. He couldn't help remembering the joy on her face when she'd gotten off the phone and given him the details.

Apparently Cassidy had thought she'd seen a girl

who went to school with her and had gone over to say hello. But the child had been farther away than Cassidy thought....

By the time she caught up to her she'd realized it wasn't her friend after all. She'd also realized something else...she was lost. Following her mother's frequent warnings not to talk to strangers, Cassidy had tried to find her way back to her aunt by herself.

Finally, scared and crying, she'd seen someone she knew she could trust. Five minutes after Cassidy had approached Mickey Mouse, she was in her aunt's arms.

Gazing down at Trish, Theo found himself overwhelmed with emotions that he had no way of deciphering. In a few short days this woman had somehow managed to worm her way into his heart. He wanted to care for her...to protect her...to love her. And to love and protect those who were important to her.

He leaned over and impulsively brushed her lips with his.

Trish smiled even before her eyes fluttered open. "I fell asleep."

Theo trailed a finger down the cheek which had been wet with tears only an hour earlier. "Yes, you did."

She sat up and stretched. "You didn't have to stay."

"I wasn't going to leave you," Theo said simply.

Trish laid her a hand flat against his cheek. "Thank you."

"My pleasure."

As Theo continued to watch her, Trish realized with sudden horror how she must look. She pushed herself to her feet, groaning as her muscles protested. "I'll be right back."

Once inside the tiny bathroom, Trish washed her face, brushed her teeth then reapplied her makeup. Despite the drops she put in them, her eyes were still red and her lids puffy. But outward appearances, Trish reminded herself, didn't matter. All that mattered was that Cassidy was safe.

When she stepped back into the main cabin, Theo was sitting out on the deck. She moved to his side and he looked up, a concerned expression on his face. "How are you doing?"

"I'm happy," Trish said, her lips curving into a smile. "I can't begin to tell you how relieved I am that my little girl is safe."

"Why don't we go to the penthouse and celebrate the good news?" Theo said. "I'll have some decadent desserts brought up. We'll put on music, have a little champagne, maybe even check out the whirlpool?"

"Sounds…heavenly." Actually it sounded like a scene tailor-made for seduction, but for some reason, the possibility didn't scare Trish anymore.

Tomorrow would be soon enough to face the real world.

Cassidy was safe.

Tonight she would celebrate.

THE NEXT MORNING Trish left Theo sleeping in the king-size bed and headed for the shower, a big smile on her face.

Last night had exceeded her wildest expectations. After dining on chocolate-covered strawberries and champagne, Theo had given her a massage intended to "relax" her. It had the opposite effect. By the time they moved on to the whirlpool, Trish had been in the mood for some serious loving.

She remembered the look in Theo's eyes when she'd removed her clothes and stepped into the whirlpool. Her body quivered as memories of last night's lovemaking washed over her. When the door to the bathroom opened and Theo stepped inside, Trish couldn't keep from smiling.

"May I join you?"

For a second Trish hesitated, feeling suddenly shy. It had been one thing to make love at night, with the lights out...

But Theo had already shown her that there was a whole new world of possibilities in life and love. By the look in his eye, the shower presented just one more possibility.

Her momentary shyness forgotten, Trish pushed the glass door open.

CHAPTER SEVENTEEN

EXHAUSTED AFTER A FULL DAY in Monte Carlo, Trish found talking to Cassidy to be energizing. It took every ounce of control not to laugh when Cassidy complained she now had to hold Aunt Angie's hand when they were out as if she was some *baby*.

After she hung up, Trish was still chuckling to herself when the phone rang again. This time it was Twyla on the line. Trish filled her in on what had happened with Cassidy and Twyla updated Trish on a couple of ongoing projects in the office. Then Twyla brought up the Liberty deal.

"How's it going?" Twyla asked. "Did Mr. Catomeris make his decision yet?"

Trish hesitated. Though Theo could change his mind—after all anything was possible—Trish knew it wasn't fair to give Twyla and James false hope.

"It's not going to be as easy as I first thought," Trish said finally. "Theo Catomeris is actually Elias Stamos's son and there is bad blood between them."

"Oh, no." Even across thousands of miles, Trish

could hear the disappointment in Twyla's voice. "At least he's agreed to think about it, right?"

"Actually he said no," Trish said. "Theo wants nothing to do with his father."

"Theo?" Twyla's tone turned curious. "Sounds like you've gotten to know him quite well."

Trish felt her face warm. "I admit it. I genuinely like the guy. That's part of the problem."

"I don't understand…"

"I know if I tell him what is at stake for me, he'll sign the contract." Trish paused, trying to unravel her tangled emotions and thoughts. "But I'm afraid if I do that, Theo would hold the fact that my business was threatened against his father and the two would never reconcile. Do you see my dilemma?"

"No," Twyla said. "Because I think you just answered your own question."

"I did?"

"You've built your business around honesty and integrity. That's why James and I wanted to work for you. You know it wouldn't be right for you to use your friendship with Mr. Catomeris for your own gain. Especially if your actions hurt him in the process."

Trish stared at the phone. In a few succinct words, Twyla had not only articulated what Trish had been trying to sort out, she'd put it in a neat little package and tied it with a bow.

"Nothing good comes from doing something immoral or illegal," Trish murmured.

"That includes exploiting a friendship for your own betterment," Twyla agreed.

"We may have to cut back for a while," Trish said. "But I promise I'll be out there drumming up new business the second the plane touches down."

"I'm not worried," Twyla assured her "We just have to have faith and stay the course."

Gratitude filled Trish's heart. What had she done to deserve such a wonderful and wise employee? "Twyla, thank you."

"For what?"

"For being such a good friend. For keeping me honest. For reminding me how lucky I am to have you and James."

Twyla laughed. "I'll remind you of that the next time we land a big account and I need a raise."

"You won't need to remind me," Trish vowed. "That raise will be yours."

The two talked for a few minutes longer, and when Trish hung up the phone, it was as if a heavy weight had been lifted from her shoulders. Her company might struggle, but it would survive.

Now Trish could only hope that Theo would find a way to reconcile with his father…on his own terms…when the time was right.

SEATED IN THE SHIP'S darkened theater, Trish cast a sideways glance at Theo. From his rapt expression it appeared that he was enjoying the Broadway Revue, too.

She had just finished speaking with Twyla when Theo stopped by after meeting with his sister. They'd had dinner in the penthouse, then headed to the theater for the late-night show. The click-clack of tap shoes brought Trish's attention back to the stage, but she couldn't concentrate. Not with Theo mere inches away.

She couldn't remember when she'd enjoyed a day more. Getting her to try parasailing in Monaco had taken a little coaxing. But once they were up and soaring, Trish's fears had disappeared.

Hanging there, high above the earth, she'd realized how long it had been since she'd done something she enjoyed just for the fun of it. Life as a single parent revolved around work commitments and Cassidy's activities.

The lights in the theater swelled, bringing Trish back to reality. She stood, still seeing the last act in her head. "Those tap combinations were fantastic."

"Are you a dancer?" he asked, rising to his feet.

"I wish," Trish said with a wry smile. "I always wanted to take lessons, but there wasn't money when I was growing up."

He was about to make a comment but Trish spoke

before he had a chance. "It probably would have been a waste anyway."

"Because?"

"Two left feet." Trish spoke matter-of-factly, hoping to forestall any expressions of sympathy. She'd had a great childhood. Her parents had given each of their five children as many opportunities as they could afford.

"You move like a dancer," Theo said. "So light on your feet."

"Puh-leeze." Trish rolled her eyes. "Have you forgotten the excursion to Kefalonia?"

"You stumbled, not fell." When she started walking, he captured her hand and tucked it firmly into the bend of his arm. "Extra support. Just in case you stumble."

The devilish twinkle in his eyes made her laugh. She was still smiling when they reached the tables and chairs grouped outside La Belle Epoque, a champagne bar and nightclub.

Theo's steps slowed. "Can I interest you in some coffee and dessert?"

Trish hesitated. She'd had Bananas Foster at dinner, but where was it written that a girl couldn't have two desserts in one day? "Cheesecake sounds good."

They'd barely gotten seated when the server took their order. He returned moments later with steaming cups of coffee and thick wedges of cheesecake covered with fresh strawberries.

Trish expelled a happy sigh. Her perfect day just kept getting better.

"Tell me." Theo wrapped his fingers around the coffee cup. "When you're in Miami, what do you do for fun?"

Trish forked a piece of the creamy confection and thought for a second. "Cassidy is the goalie on a soccer team. I love to watch her play."

Theo offered an encouraging smile.

"I also help out at Cassidy's school," Trish explained. "Organize parties for different holidays, stuff like that."

"Anything else?"

"I belong to a mother's reading group. We meet quarterly to discuss books on child rearing."

Theo took a sip of coffee. "What do you do for yourself? When you're not busy being a mother?"

Trish thought for a moment. "I used to play tennis. But time got tight and I had to quit."

"When I was a boy, my grandmother used to say it was good for me to see her making time for herself and doing something she enjoyed," Theo said in an offhand tone. "She called it 'refilling her well.'"

"And what did she do to refill this well of hers?" Trish asked.

"Genealogy research." Theo took another sip of

coffee. "I can say with the utmost confidence that there isn't a relative of ours currently alive anywhere on this earth Yiayia hasn't tracked down."

Trish wondered if he knew that his eyes lit up when he spoke of his grandparents. Or how lucky he was to have grown up surrounded by such love?

"If you could do something for yourself, what would you do?" he asked.

Trish looked up to the heavens and sighed. What was it with Theo? On this topic, he was like a dog with a bone.

"I know you're busy," Theo said. "But you could plan the activity on those nights or weekends when Cassidy is with her father."

"Why does this matter to you?" Trish asked.

"I care about you." His eyes were dark with worry. "I want you to be happy…when I'm not with you."

She finally understood. This was his way of telling her he cared…the night before he said goodbye.

THEO STARED UP at the stars, one arm crooked behind his head, the other holding Trish close. This was their last night on the ship and he'd wanted the evening to be special.

After they'd returned to the suite, he'd spread a blanket across the wooden deck floor and they'd made slow, sweet love. The moon bathed her body in a golden glow and each kiss, each caress, had taken on extra significance.

For the past few minutes, he'd simply lain next to Trish, gazing up at the stars, letting the strains of a Mozart concerto wash over him. In the quiet of the moment, Theo accepted what he'd been trying to deny…he'd fallen in love with Trish.

His heart tightened with a combination of fear and excitement. *Why* had he let this happen? *How* had he let this happen?

He tightened his arm around her and she slanted a sideways glance beneath heavy-lidded eyes. Then with comfortable familiarity she planted a soft kiss on his chest, her fingers toying with the hair on his belly.

Though it had only been a few minutes since they'd last made love, he grew instantly hard.

Her lips curved up in a smug smile. She brushed her hand over the tip and his shaft sprang forward.

"Someone is in the mood to play again," she said in a low husky voice that made his blood boil.

"Someone is always ready when you're around," Theo said, planting a kiss against her hair. It was true. Since he'd been fifteen, women had been coming on to him but never had one stirred his senses like Trish.

"You know tonight is it." Though her tone was nonchalant, he could hear a note of sadness creep into her voice. "Tomorrow we'll dock in Barcelona. I'll head back to Florida. You'll return to Corfu."

She opened her mouth as if to say more but shut it without another word.

"It's strange, isn't it?" Theo said softly.

"What?"

"Us meeting the way we did," he said. "You could almost say my father brought us together."

Trish's lips curved up in a slight smile and Theo knew she'd caught the irony in the statement.

"Where was he ten years ago?" Trish asked. "That's what I want to know."

"We were different people back then." Theo turned toward her, propping himself up on one elbow so he could see her beautiful body.

Mine, he thought with a surge of possessiveness. He knew her body as well as he knew his own…every freckle, every mole. There wasn't a single inch of her that he hadn't explored…that he hadn't kissed…or touched.

The realization was bittersweet. Soon it wouldn't matter because she'd be gone and all he'd have were memories. *No.* The word resounded in his head and his heart constricted. *I can't let her go.*

"Marry me," he said. "Move to Corfu."

His tone had taken on a certain desperation, but Theo didn't care. Right now he was desperate, panicked at losing what he'd finally found.

A look of stunned disbelief crossed Trish's face.

"I never thought," she began, searching his eyes. "I never let myself hope…"

Theo expelled the breath he didn't realize he'd been holding at her response. "You'll go back to Florida and get your things." His mind raced as he mentally checked off everything that needed to be settled before they left the ship. "My house has plenty of room. We can put in a home office if you don't want to get one in town. There shouldn't be any reason you can't run your business from Corfu. I'll—"

"What about Cassidy?" Trish interrupted, pushing up to rest on both elbows.

Theo paused. "She'd come with you, of course."

"Oh, Theo." Trish leaned over and brushed a strand of hair back from her face. "I don't know what to say."

Unease crept up his spine at the look in her eyes. "A simple yes will do."

"If only it were that easy." Regret laced her voice and his blood turned cold.

"What's the problem?" Though an arctic chill had invaded his body, Theo did his best to keep a smile on his lips and his tone light.

"Steven won't let Cassidy leave the States," she said. "And I won't leave without her."

"Ask him."

"I don't need to ask. I already know what he'll say."

She sounded so sure, but how could she know if she hadn't even talked to the guy? "He might surprise you."

"Maybe," she said, her fingers lightly stroking his arm, "you could relocate to Florida. The weather is a lot like Corfu and there's…"

"I can't." He shook his head, dismissing the option. "My grandparents are old. Other than my mother, I'm their closest relative in Corfu."

A look of such dismay crossed her face that he wanted nothing more than to pull her into his arms and tell her his grandparents didn't matter and he'd move to Florida as soon as he could get his affairs sorted out. But his grandparents had been there for him since the beginning and he loved them. He would not abandon them. "Why don't you want to ask Steven?"

"I already know the answer." Trish sat up and raked her fingers through her hair, her brows pulling together as she thought. "We'll figure something out. Cassidy and I can come to Corfu at Thanksgiving—"

"Holidays are fine but that won't solve the problem. You can't live in Corfu. I can't live in Florida." The realization was like a knife to his heart. "For a marriage to work we have to at least live on the same continent."

Trish's eyes, usually brimming with laughter, turned bleak. "We're at an impasse."

Theo clenched his jaw and nodded.

Her bottom lip began to tremble and a single tear slipped down her cheek.

Theo tightened his hands into fists at his sides to keep from reaching out to her.

"This is it then," she said in a surprisingly steady voice. "Tonight is all we have."

Theo couldn't help himself. He took both her hands in his and brought them to his lips, all the while fighting the emotion welling up inside him.

"I'm going to make tonight so good, you'll never forget me," he said with a fierceness born of pain and anguish.

"I could never forget you, Theo." Fresh tears filled Trish's eyes. "Not even if I tried."

CHAPTER EIGHTEEN

"I SENT YOU TO CORFU with a directive, Mrs. Melrose." Elias Stamos's accented voice cut like a knife. "Are you telling me you failed to accomplish the one task that you were given?"

"I approached Theo with your offer," Trish said. She'd waited until she was back in her office in Miami before calling the head of Argosy Cruises. "I encouraged him to sign. He wasn't ready."

"I understand that you and Mr. Catomeris became good friends during the cruise." Stamos paused. "I'm surprised he wouldn't do it to help you out."

"He had no idea of the possible consequences to me," Trish said.

"Why didn't you tell him?"

"When I met my first husband he wasn't ready to get married, to make that commitment," Trish said, deciding she might as well be upfront. "But I gave him an ultimatum. He didn't want to lose me so he proposed. I realize now that I pushed for something to happen before the time was right…with disastrous results."

"I assume there's a point to the story."

"The reason I didn't push Theo to sign was because I thought forcing the issue might turn him against you."

"Those horses are important to him," Stamos said. "You should have used them for leverage."

Trish bit back her frustration. Hadn't the man heard a word she'd said?

"The wild horses of Kefalonia could really benefit from your philanthropy." Showing remarkable restraint, she kept her tone even. "And if you'd choose to give a donation with no strings attached, I'd hope that Theo would accept it on behalf of the foundation. But if it's conditional, if you push, if you try to manipulate, you stand a chance of never having a good relationship with your son."

"I don't recall ever saying I wanted a relationship with Theo Catomeris," Stamos said. "Or that this was about anything other than business."

Trish could feel the chill in the words all the way from Greece. She took a deep breath and let it out.

"Have you considered the impact that losing our account will have on your bottom line?"

"Of course," Trish said. "Have you considered what *you'll* be losing? I run a good, tight operation. We've got the best tour operators signed up all over the world and we provide excellent service. If you don't want us, there are other cruise lines that do. But I hope you'll consider keeping us on."

By the time Trish hung up the phone she wasn't sure whether she'd lost the account or not. Stamos hadn't specifically said he was terminating her contract. Then again, he hadn't said he was keeping her around, either.

Though he'd kept his responses brief and succinct, a couple of times she'd felt as if he really *had* been listening.

For his sake and for Theo's she hoped he had…

Theo.

She still thought about him every day. Nights were the worst. She'd awaken convinced she could feel his hands on her body, his lips against hers.

But while she missed the physical part of their relationship, it was Theo the companion, the friend, the man, that she missed, that she loved…

The clock on the wall chimed softly and Trish glanced up, startled at the time. Everyone in the office had left hours ago. Normally, she'd have been out the door by now, too. But Steven had picked Cassidy up from school and the only thing waiting for her at home was an empty house, a freezer dinner…and thoughts of Theo. As long as she kept busy, she could keep the memories at bay.

Trish powered down her computer, grabbed her bag and rose to her feet. Maybe she'd stop by the mall, buy that pair of shoes she'd had her eye on. She'd barely taken five steps when a shrill ring split the air. Trish glanced at the phone, planning to let it go to voice mail when she saw that the call was coming in on her private line.

She hurried back to the desk and snatched up the receiver. "Trish Melrose."

"Aren't we formal?" a familiar voice on the other end of the phone teased.

"Sally." Trish plopped her bag on the desk and sat down. "How are you?"

"Fine now."

Something in Sally's voice put Trish on alert. "What's up?"

"I'm moving to Italy," Sally said with remarkable aplomb. "Next week."

"What?" Trish shrieked before lowering her voice to a more manageable level. "Tell me everything."

"It's pretty simple," Sally said. "Right after we got back from the cruise I put in for a transfer to my company's Rome office. HR called on Monday and told me the transfer had been approved."

"Rome?" Trish assumed Sally was moving because of Bruno. "Why not Naples?"

"No corporate office there," Sally said. "But Rome isn't that far. This way I'll still have an income and we won't feel that pressure to make something happen right away."

"Is Bruno happy you're moving there?"

"Ecstatic," Sally said. "Call me a hopeless romantic, but I know Bruno is my Prince Charming and we're going to be together forever."

Trish found herself smiling into the phone. "You deserve to be happy, Sal."

"So do you," Sally said. "Now tell me about Theo…any news?"

Trish's smile faded, but she forced a light tone. "What can I say? He's there. I'm here."

For several seconds Sally didn't respond.

"I've got the solution," Sally said finally. "Call him. Tell him how much you miss him. Maybe you could even fly over there and—"

"Stop," Trish said firmly. "I am not going to call or beg him to be with me."

"I wasn't suggesting you beg," Sally said. "Merely that you show him what he means to you."

"No." Trish shook her head for extra emphasis. "I care about Theo but I can't make this relationship work if that's not what he wants, too. I made that mistake with Steven. The bottom line is…he's got to meet me at least halfway."

"I WANT YOU TO BE my best man." Bruno stood by the helm of Theo's large sailboat, his two girls playing down below.

"You and Sally are getting married?" Theo

couldn't keep the surprise from his voice. He'd been shocked when his old friend had flown to Corfu for the weekend…stunned when Bruno had told him that Sally was moving to Italy.

"Not right away," Bruno said. "Sally wants to get to know the girls first."

Theo felt a swift stab of jealousy. Why couldn't Trish be the one relocating for the man she loved?

"What about Trish? I was hoping you'd have some good news of your own to share." Bruno lifted a bottle of beer to his lips, a curious gleam in his eyes.

Theo wasn't surprised at the not-so-subtle probe. The minute Bruno had shown up at his door he'd known that sooner or later his friend would bring up Trish. Theo glanced at his watch. Bruno had restrained himself for fifty-five minutes. A new record.

"Haven't heard from her." Theo lifted his shoulder in a careless shrug, the spray from the water stinging his cheeks.

He probably wasn't being fair. He hadn't called her, either. And he was the one who'd made it clear that what they'd had was over. He gave a sharp turn on the wheel.

The boat leaned to the right and Isabella and Anna squealed then giggled. "Do it again, Uncle Theo," they called. "Do it again."

Bruno eyed Theo with a speculative gaze. "I remember you being a good sailor. What happened?"

"Shut up," Theo growled.

Bruno took another swallow of beer. "Did you even ask her to stay?"

"I asked," Theo said between clenched teeth. "She said no."

Bruno had never been the most sensitive guy, but couldn't he tell Theo didn't want to talk about Trish? Even thinking about her hurt. Though Theo would never admit it, for one brief moment he'd allowed himself to hope she would stay. That she loved him as much as he loved her. That she couldn't bear to be away.

"Theo?"

Theo shoved the memories aside. He knew he had to give his friend something more substantial in order to get him to shut up. "Her ex won't allow her to take her daughter out of the U.S."

"You think she's lying?"

Theo shrugged.

A knowing glint filled Bruno's eyes. "Just as I thought. You gave up on her. Just like you gave up on your father."

The words were like a fist to Theo's belly and a slew of Greek expletives flew from his mouth.

"You push people away," Bruno continued in a matter-of-fact tone, seemingly unfazed by Theo's anger, "so they can't hurt you. You did that with your father. Now you're doing it with Trish."

The conclusion was so ridiculous Theo had to laugh. "I didn't push my father away. He's never wanted anything to do with me. Remember?"

"You could have reached out to him." Bruno glanced over to where his girls sat playing with their dolls. "He's blood, Theo. The only father you'll ever have. The older you get, the more you realize family is everything."

Easy for Bruno to say. The man had more aunts and uncles than he could count, two lovely daughters…and a woman who was willing to leave her country to be with him.

"It's not the same, Bruno," Theo said. "Elias Stamos doesn't want anything to do with me."

"He let his daughters meet you."

"They would have come anyway."

"Still, he gave his blessing."

"I'm nothing to him," Theo said, his gaze fixed firmly on the water. "Nothing."

"How do you know?" The question was direct. "Give him a call. And while you're at it, do the same with Trish. Don't be so quick to assume it won't work."

"Thank you for the advice, Doctor Tucci," Theo said in a mocking tone.

"Anytime." Bruno slid a hand into his pocket, pulled out a scrap of paper and shoved the tiny sheet into Theo's hand.

"What's this?"

"What does it look like? It's a prescription." Bruno grinned. "Sally gave me Trish's home address and phone number. Dr. Tucci says take two aspirin and call Trish in the morning."

CHAPTER NINETEEN

Two DAYS LATER Theo found himself on an elevator headed to the top floor of a five-star hotel in the heart of Athens. Bruno had barely left to return to Naples when Theo received notification that Elias Stamos had made a large donation to the foundation to help the wild horses of Kefalonia.

Theo had stared at the e-mail. Days before he'd have immediately turned down the money. But this time he'd hesitated. Not only because he knew what the sizable gift would mean to the horses, but also because, after his conversation with Bruno, the unexpected gift seemed to be a sign.

Before Theo could change his mind, he'd called Katherine and found out where Elias was staying. While Theo still wasn't sure what he was going to say to the man when they were standing face-to-face, he was no longer willing to let the past determine his future.

The elevator slowed to a stop and Theo gathered his resolve. He'd give Stamos a chance. One chance. Then no one could say he hadn't made an effort. The door slid silently open. Theo had barely taken two steps when he was confronted by two burly men in suits.

"I'm sorry, sir," the taller one said as the other silently watched. "This is a restricted access floor."

"I'm here to see Mr. Stamos," Theo said.

"Is he expecting you?" the short one asked.

"We have an appointment."

The two exchanged glances. "Your name?"

"Theo Catomeris."

The tall one punched in a few buttons then glanced down at his PDA. "Your name isn't on the list."

"We have an appointment," Theo repeated. "I'm his son."

The men hesitated, then the short, stocky one said, "I'll check. Catomeris, right?"

Theo nodded.

It couldn't have been more than a minute before the man returned. He gestured to the door. "You can go in."

The door opened into a living room that was larger than the entire first floor of Theo's small home in Corfu Town. The walls and carpet were a soft gray, and the tables and sofas almost black. A few bright splashes of color came from decorative pillows and paintings on the wall.

Elias Stamos stood looking out the window. Theo had seen him on television many times, but was unprepared for the impact of seeing him in person.

He'd convinced himself this would be a relatively cut-and-dried meeting, so the myriad of emotions that rose up in him took him by surprise. There was something about knowing this man was his own blood...

The older man turned and Theo widened his gaze, a sudden image of how he was going to look in twenty-five years flashing before him. Katherine had been right, the resemblance was amazing.

Although in his midsixties, Elias could pass for a much younger man. Well built, tanned and fit, he had a youthful handsome face and an air of confidence that came with money and power. It was a combination that Theo knew most women—including his own mother—found impossible to resist.

Elias stared for a long moment, but if he saw the resemblance or was surprised by it, his face didn't show it. "You don't look at all like your mother."

"That's what I've been told."

Stamos gestured to a large sectional. "Have a seat."

"I won't be staying long," Theo said, not giving the sofa a second glance. His emotions were raw and close to the surface, a feeling he didn't much like.

"I scheduled an hour," Elias said conversationally as if he hadn't noticed Theo's curtness.

"I wanted to thank you in person for the donation," Theo said stiffly. "It was generous and totally unexpected."

Elias's lips curved in a slight smile. "Your friend, Mrs. Melrose, is one determined woman."

Theo stood there for a moment, confused, wondering if there had been some mistake. "I didn't agree to do the excursions."

"I know that." Elias settled himself in a nearby chair and gestured to the maid who'd been standing in the background. "Single malt scotch."

When she scurried off, Theo found himself taking a seat on the sofa. "So why did you donate?"

"Like I said, your Mrs. Melrose is very determined." Elias surprised Theo with a chuckle. "Very passionate. Though I have a feeling that's no surprise to you."

Before Theo could respond, Elias continued. "She couldn't say enough about those horses and the good you're doing."

Elias's lips curved up in a wistful smile. "She reminded me of my Alexandra, so passionate but with a will of steel. My wife died, you know. Of cancer. It's been ten years and not a day goes by that I don't miss her."

The maid returned with two glasses of whiskey on a tray. Elias drank his quickly. Theo took a sip, surprised Elias had been so open about his wife.

Theo had heard all about the blond pianist from England who'd married Stamos. According to Tasia, Alexandra had been nothing more than a spoiled rich girl who'd stolen the man who should have been hers. But his mother had failed to mention one very important fact. "It sounds like you loved her very much."

Elias nodded. "Alexandra was the only woman I ever loved."

Theo met the man's gaze. "What about my mother?"

"I was no saint. I had women before I married. Lots of women." Elias gave a dismissive wave of his hand. "Your mother, she told me she was protected, taking pills so there would be no baby. But she lied. She wanted my money. That's all Tasia ever wanted...money and power."

There was disgust in Elias's tone and for a second Theo was tempted to argue, to defend his mother's reputation. But he couldn't because Theo knew what the man said was true. Wealth and its accompanying status were the only things that had ever mattered to his mother.

"You make it clear what you think of her," Theo said. "What about me?"

"I suppose you're wondering why I never came around." A tiny muscle twitched in Elias's jaw.

Theo took another sip of the scotch and waited.

"Your mother would have seen interest as a sign of weakness on my part," the older man said in a matter-of-fact tone. "She'd have used you to get to me."

It almost sounded as if his father had stayed away to...protect him? But that was crazy.

"I want to make it clear that I'm not here looking for a handout," Theo said.

"If you were after my money," Elias said, "you'd have contacted me back when you were starting your business. You wouldn't have gone from bank to bank looking for someone to loan you money."

Theo remembered that time. He'd been growing discouraged when one of the lenders who'd previously turned him down had called back and offered him the money he'd asked for at an even lower interest rate than had been previously quoted. Theo hadn't thought to question it at the time, but now…

He shot a suspicious glance at Elias but his father just signaled for the maid to bring him another drink.

"Once I became an adult, once you knew what kind of man I'd become, why didn't you contact me?"

Elias silently accepted the second glass of scotch from the maid. He stared down at the amber liquid for a long moment. "Pride," he said finally, looking up. "I hadn't been more involved when you were young. I was sure you'd be angry. I would have been in your position. In fact, I'm surprised you came here. And that you accepted my donation."

Actually, Theo was surprised, too. A month ago he'd have sent the money back. But meeting his sisters and learning of his mother's deception had made him rethink his attitude. And his time with Trish had made him realize that life wasn't always black-

and-white. His father was no saint, but Elias Stamos wasn't the monster Tasia had portrayed, either.

"I've been doing a lot of thinking these past couple of weeks," Theo said. "I realize now that while I can't control the past, I am in control of my future."

Elias tilted his head, his dark eyes watchful. "I'm not sure I understand."

"Helena and Katherine are my half sisters," Theo said. "I plan to see them again. I'd like it if we could have some sort of relationship, too."

Theo's words hung in the air as he awaited Elias's reply. But regardless of the man's decision, Theo knew he was finally charting the right course. He was going after what he wanted. Athens had been his first stop.

Next stop…Florida.

THOUGH THE STYLISHLY simple wooden benches in the observation room overlooking the dance studio were rock hard, Theo didn't mind. From this vantage point he had a perfect view of Trish and he hadn't taken his eyes off her since he'd arrived.

The instructor was making the women click their toes on the shiny floor like horses pawing the ground. The maneuver must have been more difficult than it looked because Trish was watching intently, her brow furrowed in concentration.

Dear God, he'd missed her. The longing that rose up inside him told him he'd been a fool to ever let her go.

After leaving Elias in Athens, Theo had booked the first available flight to the United States. When he'd arrived at the Miami Airport, a driver and car had been waiting, courtesy of his sister.

Theo had called Katherine before he'd left Greece to let her know that he'd met with Elias. He'd also happened to mention he was headed to Florida to see Trish. By the time he'd hung up he had access to a Liberty Line company car as well as the South Beach penthouse suite Katherine used when in Florida.

At first he'd been reluctant to accept. He wasn't sure where the relationship—if you could even call it that—with his father was headed, and using company perks seemed like trading on a fortune that wasn't his to use. But Katherine had persisted, telling him the car and penthouse were hers to offer, and if he wanted to pay her back, he could name his first daughter after her.

Theo had laughingly agreed, and now he couldn't seem to get the image of a baby girl with Trish's red hair and hazel eyes out of his head.

All the way to Miami, he'd thought about the wonderful future he and Trish could share…if she could only find it in her heart to forgive his earlier stupidity.

The flight had gone smoothly and arrived at the gate ahead of schedule. It was discovering Trish's whereabouts at six o'clock on a Wednesday afternoon that had proved most challenging. When he'd called her office from the airport, the answering service had been extremely tight-lipped.

Thankfully Katherine wasn't the only one who enjoyed a little matchmaking on the side. He'd reached Sally on her cell phone—the number being Bruno's contribution to the effort—and less than ten minutes later Theo was on his way to the studio where Trish took weekly dance lessons.

There had been laughter in Sally's voice when she'd informed Theo that Trish had joined an over-thirties beginners tap class. Theo couldn't understand her amusement. All he'd felt was pride.

"They try," the man seated next to Theo said in a conversational tone. "They just aren't very good. Which one is yours?"

Theo reluctantly pulled his gaze from Trish. "Mine?"

"You know…wife…girlfriend?" The guy gestured to the dozen women lined up on the hardwood floor below. "Sarah, my wife, is on the end. The one with the curly brown hair."

"Mine's the redhead in the middle," Theo said, the words feeling awkward on his tongue. He hoped the man didn't know Trish. Because if he did, he would know Theo was lying. Trish wasn't his…not yet anyway.

"She's cute." The words had barely left the man's mouth when he rose to his feet. "Sorry to cut this short but Sarah and I have an appointment with a Realtor. Finally going to take the plunge and buy a place of our own."

The women had begun to file out of the dance studio and Theo realized with a start that class had ended.

"Do they go out the front door?" Theo asked, following the man down the stairs to the lobby.

The man shook his head. "Sarah told me to wait by the side door. That's the exit the students use."

Theo glanced around the large ultramodern lobby. There were lots of doors. All he had to do was find the one that would lead him to Trish.

"I know where it is." The man turned back, apparently noticing Theo's hesitation. "I'll show you."

Theo wasn't sure how Trish was going to react to his unexpected appearance and he really didn't want an audience. But at the moment he didn't see any alternative.

Fifteen minutes later, Theo realized he needn't have worried. All the other women in class had left—including Sarah and her husband—and he was still waiting. He didn't know why he was surprised. On the ship he'd discovered that Trish wasn't the quickest at changing clothes or getting dressed. But then, he'd never encouraged her to hurry. He'd liked seeing her naked.

The door opened and Theo watched Trish step out into the alley. Before she could head out to the main street, he moved forward to meet her. "Hello, beautiful."

Trish rocked back on her heels, her eyes widening. She shook her head as if trying to clear her vision and blinked twice.

"Theo. It *is* you." Her voice was deep and husky and music to his ears.

"How've you been?" He didn't know why he asked. Even dressed casually in a pair of faded blue jeans and a simple cotton top, she looked fabulous. Although, on closer inspection, he could see shadows under her eyes that hadn't been there when he'd last seen her, and he realized that perfect figure of hers was now a shade too thin.

Her gaze never left his face. "What are you doing here?"

Though she'd answered his question with one of her own, Theo didn't care. They were together and talking for the first time in weeks. The rightness of his decision washed over him, sweeping away any doubt that remained.

"Don't you want to know how I've been?" he asked.

She tilted her head and the slight smile that graced her lips gave him hope. "How have you been, Theo?"

"Miserable." He took a step closer, breathing in the clean fresh scent of her. "I've missed you desperately."

Her hold on the bag in her hand faltered. Trish didn't respond immediately. Instead she settled the straps over her shoulder with inordinate care before looking back at him. "I've missed you, too."

His heart quickened. At that moment Theo wanted nothing more than to pull her to him and kiss her until she begged him to make love to her.

Only the knowledge that this trip wasn't about a night or two of passion stopped Theo from acting on the impulse. While he'd loved having her in his bed, that wasn't enough for him now. He wanted all of her. He wanted her to be a permanent part of his life. To wake up next to him every morning. To share her day with him over dinner and listen to his. "There's a café down the street. Do you have a few minutes?"

Her answer held the key to his future happiness because her response would tell him if there was any hope. Sally had mentioned Steven had Cassidy until eight o'clock on Wednesdays, which meant Trish had the time. But did she want to spend it with him?

She waited so long to answer that Theo felt his cautious optimism begin a death spiral.

"Yes," she said finally, and then again more forcefully, as if trying to convince herself. "Yes. I have time."

Theo had grown up attending church every Sunday with his grandparents. As an adult he hadn't been nearly so faithful. But this was his one chance and he hoped God was listening, because as he took Trish's arm, Theo began to pray.

CHAPTER TWENTY

TRISH'S HEART BEAT out of control and it wasn't from caffeine overload. She cast a quick glance sideways at Theo.

With his dark good looks and white cotton shirt open at the neck, he fit right in with the Miami crowd. She was fairly certain he hadn't said why he was here, although she couldn't be sure. From the moment he'd startled her outside the dance studio, a dull roar had filled her ears, making it difficult to hear.

What if I'd gone out the front door? What if I'd missed him?

She'd stayed behind in the dressing room after her classmates had left, completing a few business calls. Her goal for this week was to secure a vendor to take on the Kefalonia excursions. Elias Stamos had been surprisingly silent but she knew the man would only be patient for so long. Unfortunately, by the time Trish had finished the last call, she was frustrated and still without a tour operator. Her latest "hot" prospect hadn't been so hot in the knowledge department.

How could she hire someone who didn't even know there were horses on Kefalonia?

"Let me take that for you," Theo said, interrupting her thoughts as he effortlessly lifted her gym bag from her shoulder and swung it over his.

She smiled her thanks, and when he took her arm, a familiar heat rushed through her. She ignored the sensation. The only chance she had of getting through these next few minutes was to pretend his closeness didn't affect her.

"Is this okay?"

Trish looked up at the small coffee shop she'd passed many times on her way to the dance studio. "Fine with me."

By the time they got their coffee, Trish's tightly held control had started to slip. The scent of his cologne, the tousled curl against his forehead, even the square set of his shoulders tugged at her heart. And his mouth—perfectly sculpted and just made for...

Theo gestured to a table at the back of the café. "Do you mind if we sit back here?"

When she didn't answer or make any attempt to move, he added. "It'll be more private."

She remembered those lips on hers, on her neck, on her inner thigh...

"Trish? Your face is all red. Are you okay?"

Trish realized with sudden horror that she'd been staring at his mouth. "I'm fine," she said in a voice an octave higher than her normal range. "Back there is fine. Wherever you want to sit is fine."

For a second she thought he was about to smile, but his expression remained watchfully serious.

When they got to the table, Theo pulled out her chair then pushed it in before taking his seat. She resisted the urge to sigh.

Once seated, Trish took a sip of coffee. She relished the hot, bitter taste on her tongue, and hoped it would help clear her head. She had so many questions it was hard to know which to ask first. Basics, she finally decided. Stick to the basics. "How did you know where to find me?"

A hint of a smile crossed his face. "Sally told me."

Sally. The self-proclaimed matchmaker.

Her friend had been relentless in trying to get Trish to contact Theo and extremely disappointed at her refusal. A sudden thought struck Trish and her heart stopped. "She didn't call you, did she?"

"No," he said. "I called her."

The surprise in his eyes at the question was more reassuring to her than any words. Trish added a packet of raw sugar to her coffee, more to keep her hands busy than because she liked her drink sweetened. "You know Sally is moving to Italy."

Theo nodded. "Bruno is thrilled. He's convinced she's the one."

"Sally feels the same." Trish opened another

packet of sugar and stirred it into her coffee, finding it easier to talk about Sally's life than her own. "I'm happy they could work things out."

Theo raised a brow. "What was there to work out?"

"You know. Logistics. Him being in Italy. Her in the U.S. You have to admit that took a little planning."

"It took a willingness to make things work," he said, an expression that looked almost like regret on his face.

Was that a not-so-subtle jab at her? No, she told herself firmly. Theo understood that Cassidy made relocating to Corfu impossible. Just as she understood he couldn't leave his grandparents or his work.

Trish took a sip of her coffee and grimaced at the sweetness.

"I watched part of your lesson," Theo said. "You dance like a pro."

"Let's be honest—I suck." Trish placed her cup on the table. "Still I do enjoy it. Every week I look forward to my lesson."

"I remember you telling me you'd always wanted to learn," Theo said. "What made you finally decide to do it?"

Trish's heart had almost forgotten how it felt when Theo looked at her with such total concentration, as if everything she had to say was important to him.

"You. That day on the ship when you told me I needed to think of myself, too. That Cassidy needed to see her mother venturing out and trying new things."

"I'm surprised you remembered," Theo said.

"Are you kidding?" Trish said, before she could stop herself. "I remember everything you—"

She shut her mouth before she could say more and embarrass herself. There was absolutely no reason for him to know that she replayed every single conversation they'd ever had over and over in her head before she went to sleep at night.

"I remember, too," Theo said softly, his words like a caress.

Trish realized she'd lost control of the conversation and needed to get it back.

"Tell me, Theo, what brings you to Miami?" Trish asked in the polite tone usually reserved for strangers.

"I met my father." His dark eyes remained fixed on her.

"How did it go?"

"Well, he didn't throw me out."

For a second Trish felt a surge of pride, as if she'd personally orchestrated the reunion. Then she reminded herself she'd had nothing to do with it. She'd only planted the idea.

"I'm happy for both of you," Trish said, warmth reentering her voice. "Family is important."

Theo reached over and took her hand, his thumb caressing her palm. "That's why I'm here."

Her composure faltered at the intimate touch. Though she knew she should pull her hand away and put some distance between them, at the moment she could barely breathe, much less make any kind of movement.

"You're here because of your family?" she finally managed to stammer.

Theo's hand tightened on hers. "Because of those I want to make part of my family."

Her mouth went dry. "I don't understand."

"I love you, Trish." Theo's deep voice vibrated with emotion. "I want you to be my wife."

Though the words were almost identical to the ones he'd spoken that last night on the ship, hearing them a second time didn't lessen the impact.

"Marriage? We've been over this before." Trish was pleased she could sound so composed. "Remember? We decided back on the ship that it would never work."

"We were wrong. *I* was wrong." Theo leaned forward. "I'm here because I love you. I'm here because I'm willing to do whatever it takes to make you mine."

Her breath caught in her throat but she'd learned long ago that wanting something and making it happen were two very different things. "We have to be realistic. I checked with Steven when I got back. No way will he allow Cassidy to permanently reside outside the United States."

"You asked him?" A smile lifted Theo's lips and

he looked like a little kid who had just been given a candy store.

"I did," Trish said, concerned Theo had misunderstood. "He said no."

"If the logistics could be worked out to your satisfaction, would you do it?" Theo spoke slowly as if choosing his words carefully. "Is there room in your life for another person?"

It was a question Trish had struggled with since divorcing Steven. Before the cruise, before Theo, she'd have answered with an emphatic no. But since she'd returned to Miami she'd done a lot of hard thinking and soul searching.

"I would never shortchange Cassidy," Trish said. "But these past few weeks have shown me that it's good for her to see that I have interests of my own, things I enjoy. And if I found the right man, I believe she would see that my love for him would in no way diminish the love I feel for her."

"What about other children?" Theo asked.

"Cassidy has been begging me for a brother or sister since she was old enough to talk," Trish said with a laugh. "But that's never been an issue because I'm a bit old-fashioned. In my mind babies come after a marriage, not before."

"I totally agree," Theo said.

Of course they agreed. During their time together Trish had discovered she and Theo were in sync on all the major issues. Unfortunately that didn't matter. He lived in Corfu. She lived in Florida.

"The last night on the ship I told you there was no way we could be together," he said.

"Really, Theo—"

"But that wasn't true," he continued as if she hadn't spoken. "There's always a way if you want something enough."

Hope shot up inside of Trish but she beat it down.

"I spoke with my grandparents," Theo said. "Told them how much you meant to me. Told them that if you'd have me, I'd be moving to America. Apparently—"

Trish almost choked on her coffee but motioned for him to continue when he stopped.

"My grandmother has discovered through her genealogy research that we have family in Florida." Theo's dimple flashed. "Relatives my grandparents are eager to meet. They're already planning some vacations so they can get to know the Florida family members and spend time with me...and you."

"What about when they aren't here on vacation?" she asked. "Who will make sure they're okay?"

"I have good friends in Corfu," Theo said. "They have promised to watch over them, make sure they always have what they need."

Trish nodded, reassured. "What about your company?"

"The crew of men and women I have are very self-sufficient," he said. "However, Basil, one of the men who has been with me since the beginning, has agreed to run the business for me."

"What will you do here?" Trish asked, not meaning to grill him, but this was his future as well as hers. She needed to make sure he'd thought this through.

"I'm considering setting up a sailing operation here in Miami," Theo said. "Perhaps providing excursion services to some of the nearby islands."

"But you love Corfu…"

"I do. But it isn't going anywhere. I thought perhaps you, Cassidy and I could spend the summers there," Theo spoke quickly. "If that's not acceptable, we'll figure something else out. I meant what I said. I'm willing to do whatever it takes to be with you."

Trish was stunned. He was ready to make concessions. Ready to leave his home and business. Ready to move to a new country. Totally on his own, he'd chosen to meet her more than halfway.

Because I'm important to him. Because he loves me.

Trish's heart started to sing, but she stifled the rejoicing, still not understanding what had changed. "Why are you willing to make these concessions now when you weren't before?"

"I was afraid to take a chance on love," Theo said, "but I'm not going to let the past determine my future. That's why I'm here, begging you to give me a second chance."

"My head is spinning," Trish stammered, trying to absorb all that had been said and what it meant for her and Cassidy's future.

Theo moved around the table and pulled her to her feet, placing his hands on her shoulders. "There's no rush," he said, his voice gentle and reassuring. "No timetable. Take as much time as you need. I'm not going anywhere."

"Oh, Theo," was all she could manage as a couple tears slipped down her cheek.

"I never knew what love was until I met you." Theo brushed away the tears with the pads of his thumbs. "You are the one I was meant to be with, to grow old with, and to love for eternity."

For several seconds, she stood silent, unable to believe that what she'd wished for had finally come true. "Remember the first time we kissed?"

"How could I forget," he said, his eyes dark with emotion. "You looked like an angel in the Mediterranean moonlight."

"When I saw you, I'd just finished wishing on a star," Trish said.

"What did you wish for?" he asked when she didn't continue.

"You," she said. He wasn't going to be the only one baring his soul tonight. "I wanted you."

"For that night?"

"No," she said, her gaze never wavering. "Forever."

Theo's lips curved up in a smile and the tense set of his jaw eased.

"I've never been one for wishing on stars." Theo tilted her chin up with the curve of his finger. "Now there's no reason."

"What do you mean?" she asked, the flame of hope a roaring fire.

"I have everything I want already," Theo said as his mouth lowered, "everything I'll ever need."

His lips closed over hers and Trish realized that her days of wishing on stars were over, too. Because everything she had ever wanted was right here in her arms.

"Are you free tonight?" Trish asked after the kiss had ended, her voice more than a little breathless.

A devilish gleam filled his eyes. "What do you have in mind?"

"I'd like to take you home," Trish said. "I want you to meet my daughter."

EPILOGUE

Seven months later

THE LIGHTS OF THE CITY of Naples twinkling in the distance added a magical glow to the evening. The temperature was unseasonably warm for February, and despite the strapless dress she wore, Trish wasn't the slightest bit cold.

Sally and Bruno had been blessed with an absolutely beautiful day for their wedding. A beautiful *hectic* day, Trish thought with a rueful smile. As Sally's personal attendant as well as her Matron of Honor, Trish had been on a constant run since early morning.

Several minutes earlier, the noise level in the hotel ballroom had reached crescendo proportions and Trish had reached sensory overload. Desperate for a few moments of peace and quiet, she'd headed for the nearest exit. On the way she'd run into Sally. They'd ended up on the terrace outside Bruno's private living quarters.

"Marriage becomes you." Trish lifted her champagne glass in an impromptu toast. "You look absolutely radiant."

The smile which had been on Sally's lips since she'd seen Bruno waiting at the front of the church several hours earlier widened into a full-blown grin.

"Mrs. Bruno Tucci." Sally held out her left hand and gazed down at the sparkling diamond. "I can't help but think that if you'd hadn't invited me on the cruise, this day would never have happened. The love of my life would be in Italy and I'd still be in Omaha."

"You'd have connected somehow." Trish placed her glass on a side table. She made a broad sweep with her hand at the star-studded sky. "Your love was written in the stars. Just like mine and Theo's."

Even now Trish couldn't look at a star-filled sky without thinking of her fiancé. As she wiggled the finger with the diamond solitaire, a familiar warmth filled her. "Five more months."

"I don't understand why you're waiting so long," Sally said. "Anyone looking at you can see you're crazy about him."

"And I'm crazy about her." Theo's familiar deep voice sounded from behind Trish and a second later his arm slipped around her waist.

"I've been looking for you," he whispered against her hair.

"Just a little girl-talk," Trish said, leaning into his caress.

"She was about to explain why you two are waiting to tie the knot," Sally added.

"We thought it'd be romantic to get married on *Alexandra's Dream*," Trish reminded Sally for what she knew had to be the tenth time. "We're going to take our friends and family for a cruise on the same ship where we fell in love."

"We're going to visit the wild horses in Kefalonia—" Trish turned in Theo's arms and brought her hands to his shoulders "—and we're going to parasail in Monaco—"

"Stroll with the natives in the *passeggiata* in Lucca," Theo continued, "explore the street market in Naples—"

"Make love under the stars," Sally interjected.

Theo slanted a sideways glance at Trish and laughed. "Definitely."

At that moment Bruno strode across the deck, making a beeline for his new bride. The look in his eyes brought a lump to Trish's throat. It was all there—the love, the devotion, the till death do us part. Everything Trish had ever wanted for her best friend.

"We're talking about Theo and Trish's wedding night," Sally said, greeting her husband with a kiss.

Bruno kissed her back soundly. "I'd rather talk about my own. When are we going to get this honeymoon started?"

"I'm ready when you are, big boy." Sally trailed

a finger up his arm then stopped. "As long as the girls are settled…"

"Don't worry," Trish said. "Menka is taking good care of them. The last time I saw her she had all three tucked under her wing."

Trish hadn't been surprised when Theo's grandmother offered to take charge of Bruno's girls as well as Cassidy during the wedding festivities. On their frequent trips to Miami, Menka and Tommy Catomeris had embraced grandparenthood with gusto. Tommy had been teaching Cassidy to cook Greek cuisine while Menka was busy filling her new granddaughter's head with stories of Corfu and Greek culture.

And Cassidy was loving every minute of it. Just the other day her daughter had told Trish she'd started counting down the days until the family went to Corfu for the summer.

Family.

Trish expelled a happy sigh. Cassidy's acceptance of all things Greek extended to her stepfather, as well. Though Theo hadn't had much experience with children, it hadn't taken long for Cassidy to accept him into the tight-knit circle she and Trish shared. And recalcitrant Steven had even warmed to Theo once he'd realized that Trish's Greek boyfriend had no intentions of coming between him and his daughter.

Personally Trish thought Steven's magnanimous

mood had more to do with the fact that there was a new woman in his life. Someone he appeared to genuinely adore. They'd already told Steven to plan on bringing her to the wedding.

"Mrs. Tucci," Bruno said, a hint of urgency in his tone. "There's a problem in the honeymoon suite that has me frustrated."

Even though Bruno had an apartment at the hotel, he and Sally planned to spend the night in the hotel's elegant honeymoon suite before leaving for Venice in the morning.

A look of dismay crossed her face. "Problem?"

"Yes," Bruno said, pulling her close. "You're not there and I can't honeymoon alone."

Sally pushed back from Bruno's arms and grabbed his hand, laughing. "That's easily remedied."

"Doesn't look like he'll be frustrated for long," Theo observed, wrapping his arms around Trish as they watched the bride and groom disappear inside.

Trish snuggled against him. She loved it when Theo held her. Nestled in his strong arms she felt cherished, protected and loved.

Not a day went by that Theo didn't show her in words and actions how much he cared. Not a day went by that she didn't remember how much he'd given up to be with her. Not a day went by that she didn't feel a twinge of guilt.

"Do you ever think how much easier your life

would be if you'd fallen in love with a woman from Corfu rather than an American with a child?" Trish asked, keeping her tone deliberately light.

Theo loosened his grip on her and took a step back, holding her at arm's length. "I don't want a woman from Corfu, I want you," he said. "Having you in my life has been a blessing beyond measure. Having—"

"Still—"

"Having Cassidy has been an extra bonus," he said, not giving her a chance to speak. "I could not love the child more if she were my own flesh and blood."

"But because of me, because of *us*, you had to leave your home—"

"My home," Theo said firmly, "is wherever you are. Besides, I like living in Florida. And I have a feeling my grandparents are going to become even more frequent fliers."

"I suppose you're right," Trish said.

"You *know* I'm right." Placing his arm around her shoulders, Theo led her to a wooden bench surrounded by fragrant roses. He waited for her to sit down before taking a seat next to her and capturing her hand.

Bringing it to his lips, Theo planted a kiss in the center of the palm, curled the fingers closed and placed her hand against his chest. "You are my heart. You are my soul. There is nothing I wouldn't do for you."

His voice was husky, barely recognizable. She stared into his face, and even in the dim light there was no mistaking the love. Trish let the last little trace of guilt fade away.

How had she gotten so lucky? Never in her wildest dreams could she have imagined that the hunky Greek businessman she'd met in a Corfu taverna would become a permanent part of her life. That he would become her heart, her soul.

Her mouth curved in a smile. Best friend. Lover. And in few short months, husband.

Life didn't get any better.

* * * * *

MEDITERRANEAN NIGHTS
Join the glamorous world of cruising with the guests and crew of
Alexandra's Dream—*the newest luxury ship to set sail on the romantic Mediterranean.*
The voyage continues in September 2007 with
BREAKING ALL THE RULES
by Marisa Carroll.

Sports journalist Lola Sandler happens upon the news story of her career when she discovers that the resident golf instructor on Alexandra's Dream *is Eric Lashman. The same Eric Lashman who, four years ago, walked away from the pro-golf world and a brilliant career for a life of anonymity. But how can she betray a man she is beginning to care for so deeply?*
Here's a preview!

"ERIC LASHMAN. I've heard of you." The blonde's voice washed over him like smoke and honey. He turned his head and found himself staring into sea green eyes. Not the turquoise of the Mediterranean, but the cool, clear green of the Atlantic where he'd surfed as a teenager, always on the lookout for the great white sharks that made the coast of South Africa their home and hunting grounds. "You won the Open in—" Her eyes narrowed slightly in concentration.

"A long time ago," he said quietly. Inwardly he winced. She knew something about golf or she would have made the layman's mistake of calling it the British Open. Well. It had to happen sooner or later. He'd been on board nearly three weeks. Someone was bound to recognize him eventually.

The well-preserved matriarch held out her hand. "I'm Myra Sandler and these are my daughters, Frances, Bonnie and Lola."

Lola. That was the youngest one. The outlier. The rebel in the family, he'd bet. The name suited her.

Half ordinary, half exotic, depending on whether it was spoken in passion or in anger. She looked like that too, ordinary, wholesome in white shorts and a white shirt with a V-neck and little cap sleeves, curly blond hair pulled up in an untidy knot on top of her head. Yet the toenails peeking out of her sandals were painted watermelon pink and her dangling earrings were tiny, gold flamingos. But it was her eyes that fascinated him most. Cool, calculating on the surface, but if you looked deeply enough you could see they swirled with a kind of inner fire that hinted at passion trapped deep inside.

Eric pulled himself together. Where the hell had that come from? He never waxed poetic like that about a woman's eyes. Especially not one who was glowering at him as though she might bite his head off at any moment.

"I saw you win the Buick Open five years ago." Myra Sandler was still speaking. "I mean I watched it on television. I can't believe we're lucky enough to have you on the cruise. I've already signed up for lessons. I'm trying to talk my daughter into joining me." She motioned toward Lola with a plump hand that had a ring on almost every finger.

"I'm glad to hear that," he lied, touching the visor once more. He needed to get moving again. To get beyond the range of those curious, intelligent green eyes before she dredged up the memory of him walking off the green at Augusta that April Saturday afternoon, and that's where her thoughts were headed, he could tell. Lola Sandler, or whatever her name might be, was troubled. He could sense it with every competition-honed nerve in his body.

"I doubt they have clubs I can use," Lola said, turning her green eyes on her mother, freeing him to take a long, steadying breath.

"Lola's left handed," Myra Sandler explained. "Do you have a set of left-handed women's clubs on board?"

"I believe we do," he said, taking the chance of looking directly into those green eyes once more.

"Excellent," the mother said, beaming. Her voice seemed to come from a long way away. "I'll make sure both our names are registered immediately after lunch."

It took most of his willpower to break contact with those sexy cat eyes and turn his head toward the older woman. "I'll be at the Shore Excursion desk from two until three-thirty. We can take care of it then. Nice meeting all of you," he said, lying again, and walked away.

"Let's go. There's nothing here I want to buy and it's too beautiful an afternoon to spend inside." Lola led the way out of one of the ship's boutiques.

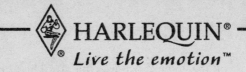

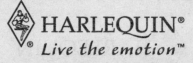

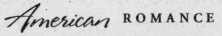
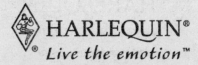

HARLEQUIN®
INTRIGUE®

BREATHTAKING ROMANTIC SUSPENSE

Shared dangers and passions lead to electrifying
romance and heart-stopping suspense!

Every month, you'll meet six new heroes
who are guaranteed to make your spine tingle
and your pulse pound. With them you'll enter
into the exciting world of Harlequin Intrigue—
where your life is on the line
and so is your heart!

THAT'S INTRIGUE—
ROMANTIC SUSPENSE
AT ITS BEST!

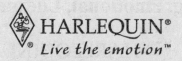

HARLEQUIN®
Live the emotion™

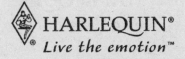